**The Revolt of Man
By Walter Besant**

PREFACE

IT is now fourteen years since this book appeared anonymously. At first the story stood cold and shivering, disregarded by the world. Six weeks, however, after its production a highly appreciative review in one of the most important journals caused people to inquire after it. Since then it has gone through many editions.

Every one who has written stories knows the unaccountable difference there is between the ease and delight of writing some and the difficulties and troubles which attend the writing of others. The Revolt of Man was written during a certain summer holiday; day by day chapter by chapter, was read out, as it was finished, to two ladies. It is needless to say that their comments on the progress of events were often most valuable. Above all I may now acknowledge their advice as to the conclusion of the story. At first it ended in a real battle. 'Let the Revolt of Man be bloodless,' said my advisers. It is bloodless. The advice was excellent, and I followed it; and now, after fourteen years, I take this opportunity of thanking them.

W. B.
United University Club;
December 1896.

CHAPTER I. IN PARK LANE

BREAKFAST was laid for two in the smallest room—a jewel of a room—of perhaps the largest house in Park Lane. It was already half-past ten, but as yet there was only one occupant of the room, an elderly lady of striking appearance. Her face, a long oval face, was wrinkled and crow-footed in a thousand lines; her capacious forehead was contracted as if with thought; her white eyebrows were thick and firmly drawn; her deep-set eyes were curiously keen and bright; her features were strongly marked,—it was a handsome face which could never, even in early girlhood, have been a pretty face; her abundant hair was of a rich creamy white, the kind of white which in age compensates its owner for the years of her youth when it was inclined to redness; her mouth was full, the lower lip slightly projecting, as is often found with those who speak much and in large rooms; her fingers were restless; her figure was withered by time. When she laid aside the paper she had been reading, and walked across the room to the open window, you might have noticed how frail and thin she seemed, yet how firmly she walked and stood.

This wrinkled face, this frail form, belonged to the foremost intellect of England; the lady was none other than Dorothy Ingleby, Professor of Ancient and Modern History in the University of Cambridge.

It would be difficult, without going into great detail, and telling many anecdotes, to account for her great reputation and the weight of her authority. She had written little; her lectures were certainly not popular with undergraduates, partly because undergraduates will never attend Professors' lectures, and partly because the University would not allow her to lecture at all on the history of the past, and the story of the present was certainly neither interesting nor enlivening. As girls at school, everybody had learned about the Great Transition, and the way in which the transfer of Power, which marked the last and greatest step of civilisation, had been brought about: the gradual substitution of women for men in the great offices; the spread of the new religion; the abolition of the monarchy; the introduction of pure theocracy, in which the ideal Perfect Woman took the place of a personal sovereign; the wise measures by which man's rough and rude strength was disciplined into obedience,—all these things were mere commonplaces of education. Even men, who learned little enough, were taught that in the old days strength was regarded more than mind, while the father actually ruled in the place which should have been occupied by the mother; these things belonged to constitutional history—nobody cared much about them; while, on the other hand, they would have liked to know—the more curious among them—what was the kind of world which existed before the development of culture gave the reins to the higher sex; and it was well known that the only person at all capable of presenting a faithful restoration of the old world was Professor Ingleby.

Again, there was a mystery about her: although in holy orders, she had always refused to preach; it was whispered that she was not orthodox. She had been twice called upon to sign the hundred and forty-four Articles, a request with which, on both occasions, she cheerfully complied, to the discomfiture of her enemies. Yet her silence in matters of religion provoked curiosity and surmise—a grave, woman, a woman with all the learning of the University Library in her head, a woman who, alone among women, held her tongue, and who, when she did speak, spoke slowly, and weighed her words, and seemed to have written out her conversation beforehand, so pointed and polished it was. In religion and politics, however, the Professor generally maintained silence absolute. Now, if a woman is always silent on those subjects upon which other women talk oftenest and feel most deeply, it is not wonderful if she becomes suspected of heterodoxy. It was known positively, and she had publicly declared, that she wished the introduction—she once said, mysteriously, the return—of a more exact and scientific training than could be gained from the political, social, and moral economy which formed the sole studies of Cambridge. Now, the Heads of Houses, the other professors, the college lecturers, and the fellows, all held the orthodox doctrine that there is no other learning requisite or desirable than that contained in the aforesaid subjects. For these, they maintained, embrace all the branches of study which are concerned with the conduct of life.

The Professor threw aside the Gazette, which contained as full a statement as was permitted of last night's debate, with an angry gesture, and walked to the open window.
'Another defeat!' she murmured. 'Poor Constance! This time, I suppose, they must resign. These continual changes of ministry bring contempt as well as disaster upon the country. Six months ago, all the Talents! Three months ago, all the Beauties! Now, all the First-classes! And what a mess—what a mess—they make between them! Why do they not come to me and make me lecture on ancient history, and learn how affairs were conducted a hundred years ago, when man was in his own place, and'—here she laughed and looked around her with a certain suspicion—'and woman was in hers?'
Then she turned her eyes out to the park below her. It was a most charming morning in June; the trees were at their freshest and their most beautiful: the flowers were at their brightest, with great masses of rhododendron, purple lilac, and the golden rain of the laburnum. The Row was well filled: young men were there, riding bravely and gallantly with their sisters, their mothers, or their wives; girls and ladies were taking their morning canter before the official day began; and along the gravel-walks girls were hastening quickly to their offices or their lecture-rooms; older ladies sat in the shade, talking politics; idlers of both sexes were strolling and sitting, watching the horses or talking to each other.
'Youth and hope!' murmured the Professor. 'Every lad hopes for a young wife; every girl trusts that success will come to her while she is still young enough to be loved. Age looks on with her young husband at her side, and prides herself in having no illusions left. Poor creatures! You destroyed love—love the consoler, love the leveller—when you, who were born to receive, undertook to give. Blind! blind!'
She turned from the window and began to examine the pictures hanging on the walls. These consisted entirely of small portraits copied from larger pictures. They were arranged in chronological order, and were in fact family portraits. The older pictures were mostly the heads of men, taken in the fall of life, gray-bearded, with strong, steadfast eyes, and the look of authority. Among them were portraits of ladies, chiefly taken in the first fresh bloom of youth.
'They knew,' said the Professor, 'how to paint a face in those days.'
Among the modern pictures a very remarkable change was apparent. The men were painted in early manhood, the women at a more mature age; the style was altered for the worse, a gaudy conventional mannerism prevailed; there was weakness in the drawing and a blind following in the colour: as for the details, they were in some cases neglected altogether, and in others elaborated so as to swamp and destroy the subject of the picture. The faces of the men were remarkable for a self-conscious beauty of the lower type: there was little intellectual expression; the hair was always curly, and while some showed a bull-like repose of strength, others wore an expression of meek and gentle submissiveness. As for the women, they were represented with all the emblems of authority—tables, thrones, papers, deeds, and pens.
'As if,' said the Professor, 'the peeresses' right divine to rule was in their hearts! But, in these days, the painter's art is a rule of thumb.'

There was a small stand full of books, chiefly of a lighter kind, prettily bound and profusely gilt. Some were novels, with such titles as The Hero of the Cricket Field, The Long Jump, The Silver Racket, and so on. Some were apparently poems, among them being Lady Longspin's Vision of the Perfect Knight, with a frontispiece, showing the Last Lap of the Seven-Mile Race; Julia Durdle's poems of the Young Man's Crown of Glory, and Aunt Agatha's Songs for Girls at School or College. There were others of a miscellaneous character, such as Guide to the Young Politician, being a series of letters to a peeress at Oxford; Meditations in the University Church; Hymns for Men; the Sacrifice of the Faithful Heart; The Womanhood of Heaven; or, the Light and Hope of Men, with many others whose title proclaimed the nature of their contents. The appearance of the books, however, did not seem to show that they were much read.
'I should have thought,' said the Professor, 'that Constance would have turned all this rubbish out of her breakfast-room. After all, though, what could she put in its place here?'
As the clock struck eleven, the door opened, and the young lady whom the Professor spoke of as Constance appeared.
She was a girl of twenty, singularly beautiful, her face was one of those very rare faces which seem as if nature, after working steadily in one mould for a good many generations, has at last succeeded in perfecting her idea. Most of our faces, somehow, look as if the mould had not quite reached the conception of the sculptor. Unfortunately, while such faces as that of Constance, Countess of Carlyon, are rare, they are seldom reproduced in children. Nature, in fact, smashes her mould when it is quite perfect, and begins again upon another. The hair was of that best and rarest brown, in which there is a touch of gold when the sun shines upon it. Her eyes were of a dark, deep blue; her face was a beautiful and delicate oval; her chin was pointed; her cheek perhaps a little too pale, and rather thin; and there was a broad edging of black under her eyes, which spoke of fatigue, anxiety, or disappointment. But she smiled when she saw her guest.
'Good morning, Professor,' she said, kissing the wrinkled cheek. 'It was good indeed of you to come. I only heard you were in town last night.'
'You are well this morning, Constance?' asked the Professor.
'Oh, yes!' replied the girl wearily. 'I am well enough. Let us have breakfast. I have been at work since eight with my secretary. You know that we resign to-day.'
'I gathered so much,' said the Professor, 'from the rag they call the Official Gazette. They do not report fully, of course, but it is clear that you had an exciting debate, and that you were defeated.'
The Countess sighed. Then she reddened and clenched her hands.
'I cannot bear to think of it,' she cried. 'We had a disgraceful night. I shall never forget it—or forgive it. It was not a debate at all; it was the exchange of unrestrained insults, rude personalities, humiliating recrimination.'
'Take some breakfast first, my dear,' said the Professor, 'and then you shall tell me as much as you please.'
Most of the breakfast was eaten by the Professor herself. Long before she had finished, Constance sprang from the table and began to pace the room in uncontrollable agitation.
'It is hard—oh! it is very hard—to preserve even common dignity, when such attacks are made. One noble peeress taunted me with my youth. It is two years since I came of age—I am twenty,—but never mind that. Another threw in my teeth my—my—my cousin Chester,'—she blushed violently; 'to think that the British House of Peeresses should have fallen so low! Another charged me with trying to be thought the loveliest woman in London; can we even listen to such things without shame? And the Duchesse de la Vieille Roche'—here she laughed bitterly—'actually had the audacity to attack my Political Economy—mine; and I was Senior in

the Tripos! When they were tired of abusing me, they began upon each other. No reporters were present. The Chancellor, poor lady! tried in vain to maintain order; the scene—with the whole House, as it seemed, screeching, crying, demanding to be heard, throwing accusations, innuendoes, insinuations, at each other—made one inclined to ask if this was really the House of Peeresses, the Parliament of Great Britain, the place where one would expect to find the noblest representatives in the whole world of culture and gentlehood.'

Constance paused, exhausted but not satisfied. She had a good deal more to say, but for the moment she stood by the window, with flashing eyes and trembling lips.

'The last mixed Parliament,' said the Professor, thoughtfully—'that in which the few men who were members seceded in a body—presented similar characteristics. The abuse of the liberty of speech led to the abolition of the Lower House. Absit omen!'

'Thank Heaven,' replied the Countess, 'that it was abolished! Since then we have had—at least we have generally had—decorum and dignity of debate.'

'Until last night, dear Constance, and a few similar last nights. Take care.'

'They cannot abolish us,' said Constance, 'because they would have nothing to fall back upon.'

The Professor coughed dryly, and took another piece of toast.

The Countess threw herself into a chair.

'At least,' she said, 'we have changed mob-government for divine right.'

'Ye—yes.' The Professor leaned back in her chair. 'James II., in the old time, said much the same thing; yet they abolished him. To be sure, in his days, divine right went through the male line.'

'Men said so,' said the Countess, 'to serve their selfish ends. How can any line be continued except through the mother? Absurd!'

Then there was silence for a little, the Professor calmly eating an egg, and the Home Secretary playing with her tea-spoon.

'We hardly expected success,' she continued, after a while; 'it was only in the desperate condition of the Party that the Cabinet gave way to my proposal. Yet I did hope that the nature of the Bill would have awakened the sympathy of a House which has brothers, fathers, nephews, and male relations of all kinds, and does not consist entirely of orphaned only daughters.'

'That is bitter, Constance,' sighed the Professor. 'I hope you did not begin by saying so.'

'No, I did not. I explained that we were about to ask for a Commission into the general condition of the men of this country. I set forth, in mild and conciliating language, a few of my facts. You know them all; I learned them from you. I showed that the whole of the educational endowments of this country have been seized upon for the advantage of women. I suggested that a small proportion might be diverted for the assistance of men. Married men with property, I showed, have no protection from the prodigality of their wives. I pointed out that the law of evidence, as regards violence towards wives, presses heavily on the man. I showed that single men's wages are barely sufficient to purchase necessary clothing. I complained of the long hours during which men have to toil in solitude or in silence, of the many cases in which they have to do housework and attend to the babies, as well as do their long day's work. And I ventured to hint at the onerous nature of the Married Mother's Tax—that five per cent. on all men's earnings.'

'My dear Constance,' interrupted the Professor, 'was it judicious to show your whole hand at once? Surely step by step would have been safer.'

'Perhaps. I ventured next to call the serious attention of the House to the grave discontent among the younger women of the middle classes who, by reason of the crowded state of the professions, are unable to think of marriage, as a rule, before forty, and often have to wait later. This was

received with cold disapprobation: the House is always touchy on the subject of marriage. But when I went on to hint that there was danger to the State in the reluctance with which the young men entered the married state under these conditions, there was such a clamour that I sat down.'
The Professor nodded.
'Just what one would have expected. Talk the conventional commonplace, and the House will listen; tell the truth, and the House will rise with one consent and shriek you down. Poor child! what did you expect?'
'A dozen rose together. Lady Cloistertown caught the Chancellor's eye. I suppose you know her extraordinary command of commonplaces. She asked whether the House was prepared to place man on an equality with woman; she supposed we should like to see him sitting with ourselves, voting with the rudeness of his intellect, even speaking with the bluntness of the masculine manner. And then she burst into a scream. "Irreligion," she cried, "was rampant; was this a moment for bringing forward such a motion? Not only women, but even men, had begun to doubt the Perfect Woman; the rule of the higher intellect was threatened; the new civilisation was tottering; we might even expect an attempt to bring about a return of the reign of brute force-" Heavens! and that was only a beginning. Then followed the weary platitudes that we know so well. Can no one place truth before us in words of freshness?'
'If you insist upon every kind of truth being naked,' said the Professor, 'you ought not to grumble if her limbs sometimes look unlovely.'
'Then let us for a while agree to accept truth in silence.'
'I would we could!' echoed the elder lady. 'I know the weariness of the commonplace. When we are every year invaded by gentlemen at Commemoration, I have to go through the same dreary performance. The phrases about the higher intellect, the sex which is created to carry on the thought, while the other executes the work of this world; the likeness and yet unlikeness between us due to that beautiful arrangement of nature; the extraordinary success we are making of our power; the loveliness of the new religion, revealed bit by bit, to one woman after another, until we were able to reach unto the conception, the vision, the realisation of the Perfect Woman——'
'Professor,' interrupted Constance, laying her hand on her friend's shoulder, 'do not talk so. Strengthen my faith; do not destroy what is left of religion by a sneer. Alas! everything seems falling away; nothing satisfies; there is no support anywhere, nor any hope. I suppose I am not strong enough for my work; at least I have failed. The whole country is crying out with discontent. The Lancashire women cannot sell their husband's work. I hear that they are taking to drink. Wife-beating has broken out again in the Potteries. It is reported that secret associations are again beginning to be formed among the men; and then there are these county magistrates with their unjust sentences. A man at Leicester has been sentenced to penal servitude for twenty years because his wife says he swore at her and threatened her. I wrote for information; the magistrate says she thought an example was needed. And, innocent or guilty, the husband is not allowed to cross-examine his wife. Then look at the recent case at Cambridge.'
'Yes,' said the Professor; 'that is bad indeed.'
'The husband—a man of hitherto blameless character,—young, well-born, handsome, good at his trade, and with some pretensions to the higher culture—sentenced to penal servitude for life for striking his wife, one of the senior fellows of Trinity!'
The Professor's eyes flashed.
'As you are going out of office to-day, my Lady Home Secretary, and can do no more justice for a while, I will tell you the truth of that case. The wife was tired of her husband. It was a most unhappy match. She wanted to marry another man, so she trumped up the charge; that is the

disgraceful truth. No fishwife of Billingsgate could have lied more impudently. He, in accordance with our, no doubt most just and well-intentioned, laws, becomes a convict for the rest of his days; she marries again. Everybody knows the truth, but nobody ventures to state it. She banged her own arm black and blue herself with the poker, and showed it in open court as the effects of his violence. As for her husband, I visited him in prison. He was calm and collected. He says that he is glad there are no children to lament his disgrace, that prison life is preferable to living any longer with such a woman, and that, on the whole, death is better than life when an innocent man can be so treated in a civilised country.'

'Poor man!' groaned Constance. 'Stay; I have a few hours yet of power. His name? she sprang to her desk.

'John Phillips—no; Phillips is the wife's name. I forgot that the sentence itself carries divorce with it. His bachelor name was Coryton.'

Constance wrote rapidly.

'John Coryton. He shall be released. A free pardon from the Home Secretary cannot be appealed against. He is free.'

She sprang from the table and rang the bell. Her private secretary appeared.

'This despatch to be forwarded at once,' she said. 'Not a moment's delay.'

'Constance!' The Professor seized her hand. 'You will have the thanks of every woman who knows the truth. All those who do not will curse the weakness of the Home Secretary.'

'I care not,' she said. 'I have done one just action in my short term of office. I—who looked to do so many good and just actions!'

'It is difficult, more difficult than one ever suspects, for a Minister to do good. Alas! my dear, John Coryton's case is only one of many.'

'I know,' replied Constance sighing. 'Yet what can I do! Our greatest enemies are—ourselves. Oh, Professor! when I think of the men working at their looms from morning until night, cooking the dinners and looking after the children, while the women sit about the village pump or in their clubs, to talk unmeaning politics—Tell me, logician, why our theories are all so logical, and our practice is so bad?'

'Everything,' said the Professor, 'in our system is rigorously logical and just. If it could not be proved scientifically—if it were not absolutely certain—the system could never be accepted by the exact intellect of cultivated women. Have not Oxford and Cambridge proclaimed this from a hundred pulpits and in a thousand text-books? My dear Lady Carlyon, you yourself proved it when you took your degree in the most brilliant essay ever written.'

The Countess winced.

'Must we, then,' she asked, 'cease to believe in logic?'

'Nay,' replied Professor Ingleby; 'I said not that. But every conclusion depends upon the minor premiss. That, dear Countess, in the case of our system, appears to me a little uncertain.'

'But where is the uncertainty? Surely you will allow me, my dear Professor,'—Constance smiled,—'although I am only a graduate of two years' standing, to know enough logic to examine a syllogism?'

'Surely, Constance. My dear, I do not presume to doubt your reasoning powers. It was only an expression of perplexity. We are so right, and things go so wrong.'

Both ladies were silent for a few moments, and Constance sighed.

'For instance,' the Professor went on, 'we were logically right when we suppressed the Sovereignty. In a perfect State, the head must also be perfect. Whom, then, could we acknowledge as head but the Perfect Woman? So we became a pure theocracy. Then, again, we were right when we abolished the Lower House; for in a perfect State, the best rulers must be those who are well-born, well-educated, and well-bred. All this requires no demonstration. Yet——'

But the Countess shook her head impatiently, and sprang to her feet.

'Enough, Professor! I am tired of debates and the battles of phrase. The House may get on without me. And I will inquire no more, even of you, Professor, into the foundations of faith, constitution, and the rest of it. I am brave, when I rise in my place, about the unalterable principles of religious and political economy: brave words do not mean brave heart. Like so many who are outspoken, which I cannot be—at least yet—my faith is sapped, I doubt.'

'She who doubts,' said the Professor, 'is perhaps near the truth.'

'Nay; for I shall cease to investigate; I shall go down to the country and talk with my tenants.'

'Do you learn much,' asked the Professor, 'of your country tenants?'

The Countess laughed.

'I teach a great deal, at least,' she replied. 'Three times a-week I lecture the women on constitutional law, and twice on the best management of husbands, sons, and farm-labourers, and so forth.'

'And you are so much occupied in teaching that you never learn? That is a great pity, Constance. Do you observe?'

'I suppose I do. Why, Professor?'

'Old habits linger longest in country places. What do you find to remark upon, most of all?'

'The strange and unnatural deference,' replied the girl, with a blush of shame, 'paid by country women to the men. Yes, Professor, after all our teaching, and in spite of all our laws, in the country districts the old illogical supremacy of brute force still obtains, thinly disguised.'

'My dear, who manages the farm?'

'Why,' said the Countess, 'the wives are supposed to manage, but their husbands really have the whole management in their own hands.'

'Who drives the cattle, sows the seed, reaps, ploughs?'

'The husband, of course. It is his duty.'

'It is,' said the Professor. 'Child, a few generations ago he did all this as the acknowledged head of the house. He does not forget.'

'What do you mean?'

'I mean, my dear Countess, that things are never so near their end as when they appear the firmest. Now, if you please, tell me something more of this great speech of yours, which so roused the wrath of assembled and hereditary wisdom. What did you intend to say?'

Constance began, in a quick, agitated way, nervously pacing the room, to run through the main points of the speech which she had prepared but had not been allowed to deliver. It was a plea for the intellectual elevation of the other sex. She pointed out that, although there was legislation in plenty for their subjection,—although the greatest care was taken to prevent men from working together, conspiring, and meeting, so that most work was done in solitude or at home—and when that was not the case, a woman was always present to enforce silence—although laws had been passed to stamp out violence, and to direct the use of brute strength into useful channels,—little or nothing had been done, even by private enterprise, for the education of men. She showed that the prisons were crammed with cases of young men who had 'broken out'; that very soon they would have no more room to hold their prisoners; that the impatience of men under the severe restrictions of the law was growing greater every day, and more dangerous to order; and that, unless some remedy were found, she trembled for the consequences.

Here the Professor raised her eyes, and laughed gently.

The Countess went on with her speech. 'I am not advocating, before this august assembly, the adoption of unconstitutional and revolutionary measures,—I claim only for men such an education of their reasoning faculties as will make them reasoning creatures. I would teach them something of what we ourselves learn, so that they may reason as we reason, and obey the law because they cannot but own that the law is just. I know that we must first encourage the young men to follow a healthy instinct which bids them be strong; yet there is more in life for a man to do than to work, to dig, to carry out orders, to be a good athlete, an obedient husband, and a conscientious father.'

Here the Professor laughed again.

'Why do you laugh, Professor?'

'Because, my dear, you are already in the way that leads to understanding.'

'You speak in parables.'

'You are yet in twilight, dear Constance.' The Professor rose and laid her hand on the young Countess's arm. 'Child, your generous heart has divined what your logic would have made it impossible for you to perceive—a great truth, perhaps the greatest of truths. Go on.'

'Have I? The House would not allow me to say it, then; my own friends deserted me; a vote of want of confidence was hurriedly passed by a majority of 235 to 22; and'—the young Minister laughed bitterly—'there is an end of my great schemes.'

'For a time—yes,' said the Professor. 'But, Constance, there is a greater work before you than you suspect or dream. Greatest of the women of all time, my child, shall you be—if what I hope may be brought to pass. Let not this little disappointment of an hour vex you any longer. Go—gain strength in the country—meditate—and read.'

'Oh, read!' cried the girl, impatiently; 'I am sick of reading.'

'Read,' continued the Professor; 'read—with closed doors—the forbidden books. They stand in your own castle, locked up in cases; they have not been destroyed because they are not known to exist. Read Shakespeare.'

Events which followed prevented the Countess from undertaking this course of study; for she remained in town. From time to time the Professor was wont to startle her by reading or quoting some passage which appealed to her imagination as nothing in modern poetry seemed able to do. She knew that the passage came from one of the old books which had been put away, locked up, or destroyed. It was generally a passage of audacity, clothing a revolutionary sentiment in words which burned themselves into her brain, and seemed alive. She never forgot these words, but she dared not repeat them. And she knew herself that the very possession of the sentiments, the knowledge that they existed, made her 'dangerous,' as her enemies called her; for most of them were on the attributes of man.

The conversation was interrupted by a servant, who brought the Countess a note.

'How very imprudent!' cried Constance, reddening with vexation. 'Why will the boy do these wild things? Help me, Professor. My cousin, Lord Chester, wants to see me, and is coming, by himself, to my house—here—immediately.'

'Surely I am sufficient guardian of the proprieties, Constance. We will say, if you like, that the boy came to see his old tutor. Let him come, and, unless he has anything for your ear alone, I can be present.'

'Heaven knows what he has to say,' his cousin sighed. 'Always some fresh escapade, some kicking over the limits of convention.' She was standing at the window, and looked out. 'And here he comes, riding along Park Lane as if it were an open common.'

CHAPTER II. THE EARL OF CHESTER

'EDWARD!' cried Constance, giving her cousin her hand, 'is this prudent? You ride down Park Lane as if you were riding after hounds, your unhappy attendant—poor girl!—trying in vain to keep up with you; and then you descend openly, and in the eyes of all, alone, at my door—the door of your unmarried cousin. Consider me, my dear Edward, if you are careless about your own reputation. Do you think I have no enemies? Do you think young Lord Chester can go anywhere without being seen and reported? Do you think all women have kind hearts and pleasant tongues?'

The young man laughed, but a little bitterly.

'My reputation, Constance, may just as well be lost as kept. What do I care for my reputation?'

At these terrible words Constance looked at him in alarm.

He was worth looking at, if only as a model, being six feet high, two-and-twenty years of age, strongly built, with crisp, curly brown hair, the shoulders of a Hercules, and the face of an Apollo. But to-day his face was clouded, and as he spoke he clenched his fist.

'What has happened now, Edward?' asked his cousin. 'Anything important? The new groom?'

'The new groom has a seat like a sack, is afraid to gallop, and can't jump. As for her nerve, she's got none. My stable-boy Jack would be worth ten of her. But if a man cannot be allowed—for the sake of his precious reputation—to ride without a girl trailing at his heels, why, I suppose there is no more to be said. No, Constance; it is worse than the new groom.'

'Edward, you are too masterful,' said his cousin, gravely. 'One cannot, even if he be Earl of Chester, fly in the face of all the convenances. Rules are made to protect the weak for their own sake; the strong obey them for the sake of the weak. You are strong; be therefore considerate. Suppose all young men were allowed to run about alone?'

The Professor shook her head gravely.

'It would be a return,' she said, 'to the practice of the ancients.'

'The barbarous practice of the ancients,' added Constance.

'The grooms might at least be taught how to ride,' grumbled the young man.

'But about this disaster, Edward; is it the postponement of a cricket match, the failure of a tennis game——'

'Constance,' he interrupted, 'I should have thought you capable of believing that I should not worry you at such a moment with trifles. I have got the most serious news for you—things for which I want your help and your sympathy.'

Constance turned pale. What could he have to tell her except one thing—the one thing which she had been dreading for two or three years?

Edward, Earl of Chester in his own right, held his title by a tenure unique in the peerage. For four generations the Countesses of Chester had borne their husbands one child only, and that a son; for four generations the Earls of Chester had married ladies of good family, certainly, but of lower rank, so that the title remained. He represented, by lineal descent through the male line, the ancient Royal House; and though there were not wanting ladies descended through the female line from old Kings of England, by this extraordinary accident he possessed the old royal descent, which was more coveted than any other in the long lists of the Red Book. It was objected that its honours were half shorn by being transmitted through so many males; but there were plenty to whisper that, according to ancient custom, the young Earl would be none other than the King of England. So long a line of only children could not but result in careful nursing of the estate, which was held in trust and ward by one Countess after another, until now it was one of the greatest in the country; and though there were a few peeresses whose acres exceeded those of the Earl of Chester, there was no young man in the matrimonial market to be compared with him. His hand was at the disposal—subject, of course, to his own agreement, which was taken for granted—of the Chancellor, who, up to the present time, had made no sign.

Young, handsome, the holder of a splendid title, the owner of a splendid rent-roll, said to be of amiable disposition, known to be proud of his descent—could there be a husband more desirable? Was it to be wondered at if every unmarried woman in a certain rank of life, whether maid or widow, dreamed of marrying the Earl of Chester, and made pictures in her own mind of herself as the Countess, sitting in the House, taking precedence as Première, after the Duchesses, holding office, ruling departments, making eloquent speeches, followed and reported by the society papers, giving great entertainments, actually being and doing what other women can only envy and sigh for?

It was whispered that Lady Carlyon would ask her cousin's hand; it was also whispered that the Chancellor (now a permanent officer of the State) would never grant her request on account of her politics; it was also whispered that a certain widow, advanced in years, of the highest rank, had been observed to pay particular attention to the young Earl in society and in the field. This report, however, was received with caution, and was not generally believed.

'Serious news!' Constance for a moment looked very pale. The Professor glanced at her with concern and even pity. 'Serious news!' She was going to add, 'Who is it?' but stopped in time. 'What is it?' she said instead.

'You have not yet heard, then,' the Earl replied, 'of the great honour done to me and to my house?'

Constance shook her head. She knew now that her worst fears were going to be realised. 'Tell me quickly, Edward.'

'No less a person than her Grace the Duchess of Dunstanburgh has offered me, through the Chancellor, the support and honour of her hand.'

Constance started. This was the worst, indeed. The Duchess of Dunstanburgh! Sixty-five years of age; already thrice a widow; the Duchess of Dunstanburgh! She could not speak.

'Have you nothing to say, Constance?' asked the young man. 'Do you not envy me my happy lot? My bride is not young to be sure, but she is a Duchess; the old Earldom will be lost in the new Duchy. She has buried three husbands already; one may look forward with joy to lying beside them in her gorgeous mausoleum. Her country house is finer than mine, but it is not so old. She is of rank so exalted that one need not inquire into her temper, which is said to be evil; nor into the little faults, such as jealousy, suspicion, meanness, greed, and avarice, with which the wicked world credits her.'

'Edward! Edward!' cried his cousin.

'Then, again, one's religion will be so beautifully brought into play. We are required to obey—that is the first thing taught in the Church catechism; all women are set in authority over us. I must therefore obey the Chancellor.'

His hearers were silent.

'Again, what says the text?—"It is man's chiefest honour to be chosen: his highest duty to give, wherever bidden, his love, his devotion, and his loyalty." '

The Professor nodded her head gravely.

'What martyrs of religion would ask for a more noble opportunity,' he asked, 'than to marry this old woman?'

'Edward!' Constance could only warn. She sees no way to advise. 'Do not scoff.'

'Let us face the position,' said the Professor. 'The Chancellor has gone through the form of asking your consent to this marriage. When?'

'Last night.'

'And when do you see her?'

'I am to see her ladyship this very morning.'

'To inform her of your acquiescence. Yes; it is the usual form. The time is very short.'

'My acquiescence?' asked the Earl. 'We shall see about that presently.'

'Patience, my lord!' The Professor was thinking what to advise for the best. 'Patience! Let us have no sudden and violent resolves. We may get time. Ay—time will be our best friend. Remember that the Chancellor must be obeyed. She may, for the sake of courtesy, go through the form of proposing a suitable alliance for your consideration, but her proposition is her order, which you must obey. Otherwise it is contempt of court, and the penalty——'

'I know it,' said the Earl, 'already. It is imprisonment.'

'Such contempt would be punished by imprisonment for life. Imprisonment, hopeless.'

'Nay,' he replied. 'Not hopeless, because one could always hope in the power of friends. Have I not Constance? And then, you see, Professor, I am two-and-twenty, while the Chancellor and the Duchess are both sixty-five. Perhaps they may join the majority.'

The Professor shook her head. Even to speak of the age of so great a lady, even to hint at her death as an event likely to happen soon, was an outrage against propriety—which is religion.

'My determination is this,' he went on, 'whatever the consequence, I will never marry the Duchess. Law or no law, I will never marry a woman unless I love her.' His eye rested for a moment on his cousin, and he reddened. 'I may be imprisoned, but I shall carry with me the sympathy of every woman—that is, of every young woman—in the country.'

'That will not help you, poor boy,' said the Professor. 'Hundreds of men are lying in our prisons who would have the sympathies of young women, were their histories known. But they lie there still, and will lie there till they die.'

'Then I,' said the Earl proudly, 'will lie with them.'

There were moments when this young man seemed to forget the lessons of his early training, and the examples of his fellows. The meekness, modesty, submission, and docility which should mark the perfect man sometimes disappeared, and gave place to an assumption of the authority which should only belong to woman. At such times, in his own castle, his servants trembled before him; the stoutest woman's heart failed for fear: even his guardian, the Dowager Lady Boltons, selected carefully by the Chancellor on account of her inflexible character, and because she had already reduced to complete submission a young heir of the most obstinate disposition, and the rudest and most uncompromising material, quailed before him. He rode over her, so to speak. His will conquered hers. She was ashamed to own it; she did not acquaint the Chancellor with her ward's masterful character, but she knew, in her own mind, that her guardianship had been a failure. Nay, so strange was the personal influence of the young man, so infectious among the men were such assertions of will, that any husband who happened to witness one of them, would go home and carry on in fashion so masterful, so independent, and so self-willed, even those who had previously been the most submissive, that they were only brought to reason and proper submission by threats, remonstrances, and visits of admonition from the vicar—who, poor woman, was always occupied in the pulpit, owing to the Earl's bad example, with the disobedience of man and its awful consequences here and hereafter. Sometimes these failed. Then they became acquainted with the inside of a prison and with bread and water.

'Let us get time,' said the Professor. 'My lord, I hope,'—here she sunk her voice to a whisper—'that you will neither lie in a prison nor marry any but the woman you love.'

Again the young man's eyes boldly fell upon Constance, who blushed without knowing why. Then the Professor, without any excuse, left them alone.

'You have,' said Lord Chester, 'something to say to me, Constance.'

She hesitated. What use to say now what should have been said at another time and at a more fitting opportunity?

'I am no milky, modest, obedient youth, Constance. You know me well. Have you nothing to say to me?'

In the novels, the young man who hears the first word of love generally sinks on his knees, and with downcast eyes and blushing face reverentially kisses the hand so graciously offered to him. In ordinary life they had to wait until they were asked. Yet this young man was actually asking—boldly asking—for the word of love—what else could he mean?—and instead of blushing, was fixedly regarding Constance with fearless eyes.

'It seems idle now to say it,' she replied, stammering and hesitating—though in novels the woman always spoke up in a clear, calm, and resolute accents; 'but, Edward, had the Chancellor not been notoriously the personal friend and creature of the Duchess, I should have gone to her long ago. They were schoolfellows; she owes her promotion to the Duchess; she would most certainly have rewarded her Grace by refusing my request.'

'Yet you are a Carlyon and I am a Chester. On what plea?'

'Cousinship, incompatibility of temper, some legal quibble—who knows? However, that is past; forget, my poor Edward, that I have told what should have been a secret. You will marry the Duchess—you——'

He interrupted her by laughing—a cheerfully sarcastic laugh, as of one who holds the winning cards and means to play them.

'Fair cousin,' he said, 'I have something to say to you of far more importance than that. You have retired before an imaginary difficulty. I am going to face a real difficulty, a real danger. Constance,' he went on, 'you and I are such old friends and playfellows, that you know me as well as a woman can ever know a man who is not her husband. We played together when you were three and I was five. When you were ten and I was twelve, we read out of the same book until the stupidity and absurdity of modern custom tried to stop me from reading any more. Since then we have read separately, and you have done your best to addle your pretty head with political economy, in the name and by the aid of which you and your House of Lawmakers have ruined this once great country.'

'Edward! this is the wildest treason. Where, oh, where, did you learn to talk—to think—to dare such dreadful things?'

'Never mind where, Constance. In those days—in those years of daily companionship—a hope grew up in my heart,—a flame of fire which kept me alive, I think, amidst the depression and gloom of my fellow men. Can you doubt what was that hope?'

Constance trembled—the Countess of Carlyon, the Home Secretary, trembled. Had she ever before, in all her life, trembled? She was afraid. In the novels, it was true, many a young man, greatly daring, by a bold word swept away a cloud of misunderstanding and reserve. But this was in novels written by women of the middle class, who can never hope to marry young, for the solace of people of their own rank. It was not to be expected that in such works there should be any basis of reality—they were in no sense pictures of life; for, in reality, as was deplored almost openly, when these elderly ladies were rich enough to take a husband and face the possibilities of marriage, though they always chose the young men, it was rare indeed that they met with more than a respectful acquiescence. Nothing, ladies complained, among each other, was more difficult to win and retain a young man's love. But here was this headstrong youth, with love in his eyes—bold, passionate, masterful love—overpowering love—love in his attitude as he bent over the girl, and love upon his lips. Oh, dignity of a Home Secretary! Oh, rules and conventions of life! Oh, restraints of religion! Where were they all at this most fatal moment?

'Constance,' he said taking her hand, 'all the rubbish about manly modesty is outside the door: and that is closed. I am descended from a race who in the good old days wooed their brides for themselves, and fought for them too, if necessary. Not toothless, hoary old women, but young, sunny, blooming girls, like yourself. And they wooed them thus, my sweet.' He seized her in his strong arms and kissed her on the lips, on the cheeks, on the forehead. Constance, frightened and moved, made no resistance, and answered nothing. Once she looked up and met his eyes, but they were so strong, so burning, so determined, that she was fain to look no longer. 'I love you, my dear,' the shameless young man went on,—'I love you. I have always loved you, and shall never love any other woman; and if I may not marry you, I will never marry at all. Kiss me yourself, my sweet; tell me that you love me.'

Had he a spell? was he a wizard, this lover of hers? Could Constance, she thought afterwards, trying to recall the scene, have dreamed the thing, or did she throw her arms about his neck and murmur in his ears that she too loved him, and that if she could not marry him, there was no other man in all the world for her?

To recall those five precious minutes, indeed, was afterwards to experience a sense of humiliation which, while it crimsoned her cheek, made her heart and pulse to beat, and sent the blood coursing through her veins. She felt so feeble and so small, but then her lover was so strong. Could she have believed it possible that the will of a man should thus be able to overpower her? Why, she made no resistance at all while her cousin in this unheard-of manner betrayed a passion which ... which ... yes, by all the principles of holy religion, by all the rules of society, by all the teaching which inculcated submission, patience, and waiting to be chosen, caused this young man to deserve punishment—condign, sharp, exemplary. And yet—what did this mean? Constance felt her heart go forth to him. She loved him the more for his masterfulness; she was prouder of herself because of his great passion.

That was what she thought afterwards. What she did, when she began to recover, was to free herself and hide her burning face in her hands.

'Edward,' she whispered, 'we are mad. And I, who should have known better, am the more culpable. Let us forget this moment. Let us respect each other. Let us be silent.'

'Respect?' he echoed. 'Why, who could respect you, Constance, more than I do? Silence? Yes, for a while. Forget? Never!'

'It is wrong, it is irreligious,' she faltered.

'Wrong! Oh, Constance, let us not, between ourselves, talk the foolish unrealities of school and pulpit.'

'Oh, Edward!'—she looked about her in terror—'for Heaven's sake do not blaspheme. If any were to hear you. For words less rebellious men have been sent to the prisons for life.'

He laughed. This young infidel laughed at law as he laughed at religion.

'Have patience,' Constance went on, trying to get into her usual frame of mind; but she was shaken to the very foundation, and at the moment actually felt as if her religion was turned upside down and her allegiance transferred to the Perfect Man. 'Have patience, Edward; you will yet win through to the higher faith. Many a young man overpowered by his strength, as you have been, has had his doubts, and yet has landed at last upon the solid rock of truth.'

Edward made no reply to this, not even by a smile. It was not a moment in which the ordinary consolations of religion, so freely offered by women to men, could touch his soul. He took out his watch and remarked that the time was getting on, and that the Chancellor's appointment must be kept.

'With her ladyship, I suppose,' he said, 'we shall find the painted, ruddled, bewigged old hag who has the audacity to ask me—me—in marriage.'

Constance caught his hand.

'Edward! cousin! are you mad? Are you proposing to seek a prison at once? Hag? old? painted? ruddled? And this of the Duchess of Dunstanburgh? Are you aware that the least of these charges is actionable at common law? For my sake, Edward, if not your own, be careful.'

'I will, sweet Constance. And for your sake, just to our two selves, I repeat that the painted——'

'Oh!'

'The ruddled——'

'Oh, hush!'

'The bewigged——'

'Edward!'

'Old hag—do you hear?—OLD HAG shall never marry me.'

Once more this audacious and unmanly lover, who respected nothing, seized her by the waist and kissed her lips. Once more Lady Carlyon felt that unaccountable weakness steal upon her, so that she was bewildered, faint, and humiliated. For a moment she lay still and acquiescent in his arms. Worse than all, the door opened and Professor Ingleby surprised her in this compromising situation.

'Upon my word!' she said, with a smile upon her lips; 'upon my word, my lord—Constance—if her Grace of Dunstanburgh knew this! Children, children!'—she laid her withered hand upon Constance's head—'I pray that this thing may be. But we want time. Let us keep Lord Chester's appointment. And, as far as you can, leave to me, my lord, your old tutor, the task of speech. I know the Duchess, and I know the Chancellor. It may be that the oil of persuasion will be more efficacious than the lash of contradiction. Let me try.'

They stood confused—even the unblushing front of the lover reddened.

'I have thought of a way of getting time. Come with us, Constance, as Lord Chester's nearest female relation; I as his tutor, in absence of Lady Boltons, who is ill. When the Chancellor proposes the Duchess, do you propose—yourself. She will decide against you on the spot. Appeal to the House; that will give us three months' delay.'

CHAPTER III. THE CHANCELLOR

THE CHANCELLOR, a lady now advanced in years, was of humble origin—a fact to which she often alluded to at public meetings with a curious mixture of humility and pride: the former, because it did really humiliate her in a country where so much deference was paid to hereditary rank, to reflect that she could not be proud of her ancestors; the latter, because her position was really so splendid, and her enemies could not but acknowledge it. She had plenty of enemies—as was, of course, the case with every successful woman in every line of life—and these were unanimous in declaring that she proclaimed her humble origin only because, if she attempted to conceal it, other people would proclaim it for her. And, indeed, without attributing extraordinary malice to these ladies, the Chancellor's unsuccessful rivals and enemies, this statement was probably true—nothing being more common, during an animated debate, than for the ladies to hurl at each other's heads all such facts procurable as might be calculated to damage the reputation of a family: and this so much so, that after a lively night the family trees were as much scotched, broken, and lopped as a public pleasure-garden in the nineteenth century after the first Monday in August.

At this time the Chancellor had arrived at a respectable age—being, that is to say, in her sixty-sixth year. She was a woman of uneven temper, having been soured by a long life of struggle against rivals who lost no opportunity of assailing her public and private reputation. She had remained unmarried, because, said her foes, no man would consent to link his lot with so spiteful a person; she was no lawyer, they said, because her whole desire and aim had been to show herself a lawyer of the highest rank; she was partial—this they said for the same reason, because she wanted to be remembered as an upright judge. They alluded in the House to her ignorance of the higher culture—although the poor lady had taught herself half-a-dozen languages, and was skilled in many arts; and they taunted her with her friendship for, meaning her dependence upon, her patron, the Duchess of Dunstanburgh. The last accusation was the burr that stuck, because the poor Chancellor could not deny its truth. She was, in fact, the daughter of a very respectable woman—a tenant-farmer of the Duchess. Her Grace found the girl clever, and educated her. She acquired over her, by the force of her personal character, an extraordinary influence—having made her entirely her own creature. She found the money for her entrance at the Bar, pushed her at the beginning, watched her upward course, never let her forget that everything was owing to her own patronage at the outset, and, when the greatest prize of the profession was in her grasp, and the farmer's girl became Chancellor, the Duchess of Dunstanburgh—by one of those acts of hers which upset the debates and resolutions of years—passed a Bill which made the appointment tenable for life, and so transferred into her own hands all the power, all the legal skill of the Chancellor. It was the most brilliant political coup ever made. Those who knew whispered that the Chancellor had no voice, no authority, no independent action at all; her patron regulated everything. While this terrible Duchess lived, the Court of Chancery belonged to her with all its manifold and complicated powers. She herself was, save at rare intervals, Prime Minister, Autocrat, and almost Dictator. Certainly it was notorious that whatever the Duchess of Dunstanburgh wanted she had; and it was also a fact not to be disputed, that there were many lawyers of higher repute, more dignified, more learned, more eloquent, and of better birth, who had been passed over to make room for this protégée of the Duchess—this 'daughter of the plough.'

Lord Chester, accompanied by the Countess of Carlyon and Professor Ingleby, arrived at the Law Courts at twelve, the hour of the Chancellor's appointment, and were shown into an ante-room. Here, with a want of courtesy most remarkable, considering the rank of the ward in Chancery whose future was to be decided at this interview, they were kept waiting for half an hour. When at length they were admitted to the presence, they were astonished to find that, contrary to all precedent, the Duchess of Dunstanburgh herself was with the Chancellor. In fact she had been directing her creature in the line she was to take: she intended to receive the hand of the Earl from her, and to push on the marriage without an hour's delay. It was sharp practice; but her Grace was not a woman who considered herself bound by the ordinary rules. Any lesser person would have made her petition for the hand of a ward, and waited until she had received in due course official notification of acceptance, when an interview would have been arranged and the papers signed. All this, owing to the delays of Chancery, generally took from a twelvemonth upwards; and in the case of poor people who had no interest, perhaps their petitions were never decided at all, so that the unfortunate petitioner waited in vain, until she died of old age, still unmarried; and the unlucky ward lived on, hoping against hope, till his time for marriage went by. The Duchess possessed even more than the dignity which became her rank. She was rather a tall woman, with aquiline features; her age was sixty-five, and in her make-up she studiously affected, not the bloom and elasticity of youth, but the vigour and strength of middle life—say of fifty. All the resources of art were lavished upon her with this object: her hair showed a touch of gray upon the temples, but was still abundant, rich, and glossy, and was so beautifully arranged that it challenged the admiration even of those who knew that it was a wig; her eyebrows were dark and well defined—her enemies said she kept a special artist continually employed in making new eyebrows; her teeth were of pearly whiteness; her cheeks, just touched with paint, showed none of the wrinkles of time—though no one knew how that was managed; her forehead strong and broad, was crossed by three deep lines which could not be effaced by any artist. Some said they were caused by the successive deaths of three husbands, and therefore marked the Duchess's profound grief and the goodness of her heart, because it was known that one of them at least—the third, youngest, and handsomest of all, upon whom the fond wife lavished all her affections—had given her the greatest trouble; indeed, it was even said that—and that—and that—with many other circumstances showing the blackest ingratitude, so that women held up their hands and wondered what men wanted. But her Grace's enemies said that her famous wrinkles were caused by her three great vices of pride, ambition, and avarice; and they declared that if she developed another such furrow, it would represent her other great vice of vanity. As for that third husband—could one expect the poor young man to fall in love with a woman already fifty-eight when she married him?

The Duchess was richly but plainly dressed in black velvet and lace; her figure was still full. As she rose to greet the Chancellor's ward, she leaned upon a gold-headed stick—being somewhat troubled with gout. Her smile was encouraging and kind towards the Earl; to Constance, as to a political enemy who was to be treated with all external courtesy, she bowed low; and she coldly inclined her head in return to the profound act of deference paid to her by the Professor. The Chancellor, a fussy little woman with withered cheeks, wrinkled brow, and thin gray locks, sat at her table. She hardly rose to greet her ward, whom she motioned to a chair. Then she looked at Constance, and waited for her to explain her presence.

'I come with Lord Chester on this occasion,' said Constance, 'as his nearest female relation. As your ladyship is probably aware, I am his second cousin.'

The Chancellor bowed. Then the Professor spoke.

'I ask your ladyship's permission to appear in support of my pupil on this important occasion. His guardian, Lady Boltons, is unfortunately too ill to be present.'

'There is no reason, I suppose,' said the Chancellor, ungraciously, and with a glance of some anxiety at the Duchess, 'why you should not be present, Professor Ingleby;—unless, that is, the Earl of Chester would rather see me alone. But the proceedings are most formal.'

Lord Chester, who was very grave, merely shook his head. Then the Chancellor shuffled about her papers for a few moments, and addressed her ward.

'Your lordship will kindly give me your best attention,' she began, with some approach to blandness. 'I am glad, in the first place, to congratulate you on your health, your appearance, and your strength. I have received the best reports on your moral and religious behaviour, and your docility, and—and—so on, from your guardian, Lady Boltons, and I am only sorry that she is not able to be here herself, in order to receive from me my thanks for the faithful and conscientious discharge of her duties, and from the Duchess of Dunstanburgh a recognition of her services in those terms which come from no one with more weight and more dignity than from her Grace.'

The Duchess held up a hand in deprecation; the Professor nodded, and lifted up her hands and smiled, as if a word of thanks from the Duchess was all she, for her part, wanted, in order to be

perfectly happy. The Earl, one is sorry to say, sat looking straight at the Chancellor without an expression of any kind, unless it were one of patient endurance. The Chancellor went on.
'You will shortly, you now know, pass from my guardianship to the hands and care of another far more able and worthy to hold the reins of authority than myself.'
Here Constance rose.
'Before your ladyship goes any further, I beg to state to you that Lord Chester has only this morning informed me of a proposal made to you by her Grace of Dunstanburgh, which is now under your consideration.'
'It certainly is,' said the Chancellor, 'and I am about——'
'Before you proceed,'—Constance changed colour, but her voice was firm,—'you will permit me also to make official and formal application in the presence of the Duchess herself, who will, I am sure, be a witness, and Professor Ingleby, for the hand of Lord Chester. There is, I think, no occasion for me to say anything in addition to my simple proposal. What I could add would probably not influence your ladyship's decision. You know me, and all that is to be known about me——'
'This is most astonishing!' cried the Duchess.
'May I ask your Grace what is astonishing about this proposal? May I remind you that I have known Lord Chester all my life; that we are equals in point of rank, position, and wealth; that I am, if I may say so, not altogether undistinguished, even in the House of which your Grace is so exalted an ornament? But I have to do with the judgment of your ladyship, not the opinion of the Duchess.'
The Chancellor turned anxiously to her patroness, as if for direction. She replied with dignity.
'Your ladyship is aware that, as the earlier applicant, my proposal would naturally take precedence in your ladyship's consideration of any later ones. I might even demand that it be considered on its own merits, without reference at all to Lady Carlyon's proposal, with regard to which I keep my own opinion.'
Constance remarked, coldly, that her Grace's opinion was unfortunately, in most important matters, exactly opposite to her own and to that of her friends, and she was contented to disagree with her. She then informed the Chancellor that as no decision had been given as to the marriage of Lord Chester, the case was still before her, and, she submitted, the proposals both of herself and of the Duchess should be weighed by her ladyship. 'And,' she added, 'I would humbly submit that there are many other considerations, in the case of so old and great a House as that represented by Lord Chester, which should be taken account of. Higher rank than his own, for instance, need not be desired, nor greater wealth; nor many other things which in humbler marriages may be considered. I will go further: in this room, which is, as it were, a secret chamber, I say boldly that care should be taken to continue so old and illustrious a line.'
'And why,' cried the Duchess sharply, and dropping her stick—'why should it not be continued?'
Here a remarkable thing happened. Lord Chester should have affected a complete ignorance of the insult which Constance had deliberately flung in her rival's teeth: what he did do was to turn slowly round and stare, in undisguised wonder, at the Duchess, as if surprised at her audacity. Even her Grace, with all her pride and experience, could not sustain this calm, cold look. She faltered and said no more. Lord Chester picked up the stick, and handed it to her with a low bow.
'I am much obliged to you, Lady Carlyon,' said the Chancellor, tapping her knuckles with her glasses; 'very much obliged to you, I am sure, for laying down rules for my guidance—MINE!—in the interpretation of the law and my duty. That, however, may pass. It is my business—

although I confess that this interruption is of a most surprising and unprecedented nature—to proceed with the case before me, which is that of the proposal made by the Duchess of Dunstanburgh.'

'Do I understand,' asked Lady Carlyon, 'that you refuse to receive my proposal? Remember that you must receive it. You cannot help receiving it. This is a public matter, which shall, if necessary, be brought before the House and before the nation. I say that your ladyship must receive my proposal.'

'Upon my word!' cried the Chancellor. 'Upon my word!'

'Perhaps,' said the Duchess, 'if Lady Carlyon's proposal were to be received—let me ask that it may be received, even if against precedent—the consideration of the case could be proceeded with at once, and perhaps your ladyship's decision might be given on the spot.'

'Very good—very good.' The Chancellor was glad to get out of a difficulty. 'I will take the second proposal into consideration as well as the first. Now then, my Lord. You have been already informed that the Duchess has asked me for your hand.'

Here the Duchess made a gesture, and slowly rose, as if about to speak. 'A proposition of this kind,' she said, in a clear and firm voice, 'naturally brings with it, to any young man, and especially a young man of our Order, some sense of embarrassment. He has been taught—that is' (here she bent her brows and put on her glasses at the Professor, who was bowing her head at every period, keeping time with her hands, as if in deference to the words of the Duchess, and as if they contained truths which could not be suffered to be forgotten), 'if he has been properly taught—the sacredness of the marriage state, the unworthiness of man, the duties of submission and obedience, which, when rightly carried out, lead to the higher levels. And in proportion to the soundness of his training, and the goodness of his heart, is he embarrassed when the time of his great happiness arrives.' The Professor bowed, and spread her hands as if in agreement with so much wisdom so beautifully expressed. 'Lord Chester,' continued the Duchess, 'I have long watched you in silence; I have seen in you qualities which, I believe, befit a consort of my rank. You possess pride of birth, dexterity, skill, grace; you know how to wield such authority as becomes a man. You will exchange your earl's coronet for the higher one of a duke. I am sure you will wear it worthily. You will——' Here Constance interrupted.

'Permit me, your Grace, to remind you that the Chancellor's decision has not yet been given.'

The Duchess sat down frowning. This young lady should be made to feel her resentment. But for the moment she gave way and scowled, leaning her chin upon her stick. It was a hard face even when she smiled; when she frowned it was a face to look upon and tremble.

The Chancellor turned over her papers impatiently.

'I see nothing,' she said.—'I see nothing at all in the proposition made by Lady Carlyon to alter my opinion, previously formed, that the Duchess has made an offer which seems in every way calculated to promote the moral, spiritual, and material happiness of my ward.'

'May I ask,' said Lord Chester quietly, 'if I may express my own views on this somewhat important matter?'

'You?' the Chancellor positively shrieked. 'You? The ignorance in which boys are brought up is disgraceful! A ward in Chancery to express an opinion upon his own marriage! Positively a real ward in Chancery! Is the world turning upside down?'

The audacity of the remark, and the happy calmness with which it was proffered, were irresistible. All the ladies, except the Chancellor, laughed. The Duchess loudly. This little escapade of youth and ignorance amused her. Constance laughed too, with a little pity. The Professor laughed with some show of shame, as if Lord Chester's ignorance reflected in a

manner upon herself.
Then the Chancellor went on again with some temper.
'Let me resume. It is my duty to consider nothing but the interests of my ward. Very good. I have considered them. My Lord Chester, in giving your hand to the Duchess of Dunstanburgh, I serve your best and highest interests. The case is decided. There is no more to be said.'
'There is, on the contrary, much more to be said,' observed Constance. 'I give your ladyship notice of appeal to the House of Peeresses. I shall appeal to them, and to the nation through them, whether your decision in this case is reasonable, just, and in accordance with the interests of your ward.'
This was, indeed, a formidable threat. An appeal to the House meant, with such fighting-power as Constance and her party, although a minority, possessed, and knew how to direct, a delay of perhaps six months, even if the case came on from day to day. Even the practised old Duchess, used to the wordy warfare of the House, shrank from such a contest.
'You will not, surely, Lady Carlyon,' she said, 'drag your cousin's name into the Supreme Court of Appeal.'
'I certainly will,' replied Constance.
'It will cost hundreds of thousands, and months—months of struggle.'
'As for the cost, that is my affair; as for the delay, I can wait—perhaps longer than your Grace.'
The Duchess said no more. Twice had Lady Carlyon insulted her. But her revenge would wait.
'We have already,' she said, 'occupied too much of the Chancellor's valuable time. I wish your ladyship good morning.'
Lord Chester offered his arm.
'Thank you,' she said accepting it, 'as far as the carriage-door only, for the present. I trust, my lord, that before long you will have the right to enter the carriage with me. Meanwhile, believe me, that it is not through my fault that your name is to be made the subject of public discussion. Pending the appeal, let us not betray, by appearing together, any feeling other than that of pure friendship. And I hope,' viciously addressing Constance, 'that you, young lady, will observe the same prudence.'
Constance simply bowed and said nothing. The Chancellor rose, shook hands with her ward, and retired.
The Duchess leaned upon the strong arm which led her to her carriage, and kissed her hand in farewell to the young man with so much affection and friendly interest that it was beautiful to behold. After this act of politeness, the young man returned to Constance.
'Painted——' he began.
'Edward, I will not allow it. Silence, sir! We part here for the present.'
'Constance,' he whispered, 'you will not forget—all that I said?'
'Not one word,' she replied with troubled brow. 'But we must meet no more for a while.'
'Courage!' cried the Professor, 'we have gained time.'

CHAPTER IV. THE GREAT DUCHESS

IMPOSSIBLE, of course, that so important a case as the appeal of Lady Carlyon should be concealed. In fact Constance's policy was evidently to give it as much publicity as possible. She rightly judged that although, in her own Order, and in the House, which has to look at things from many points of view, motives of policy might be considered sufficient to override sentimental objections, and it was not likely that much weight would be attached to a young man's feelings; yet the Duchess had many enemies, even on her own side of the House—private enemies wounded by her pride and insolence—who would rejoice at seeing her meet with a check in her self-willed and selfish course. But, besides the House, there was the outside world to consider. There was never greater need on the part of the governing caste for conciliation and respect to public opinions than at this moment—a fact perfectly well understood by all who were not blind to the meaning of things current. The abolition of the Lower House, although of late years it had degenerated into something noisier than a vestry, something less decorous than a school-board in which every woman has her own hobby of educational methods, had never been a popular act. A little of the old respect for so ancient a House still survived,—a little of the traditional reverence for a Parliament which had once protected the liberties of the people, still lingered in the hearts of the nation. The immediate relief, it is true, was undoubtedly great when the noise of elections—which never ceased, because the House was continually dissolved—the squabbles about corruption, the scandals in the House itself, the gossip about the jobs perpetrated by the members, all ceased at once, and as if by magic the country became silent; yet the pendulum of opinion was going back again—women who took up political matters were looking around for an outlet to their activity, and were already at their clubs asking awkward questions about what they had gained by giving up all the power to hereditary legislators. Nor did the old plan of sending round official orators to lecture on the advantages of oligarchical and maternal government seem to answer any longer. The women who used to draw crowded audiences and frantic applause as they depicted and laid bare the scandals and miseries and ridiculous squabbles of the Lower House, who pointed to session after session consumed in noisy talk, now shouted to empty benches, or worse still, benches crowded with listless men, who only sat bored with details in which they were forbidden to take any part, and therefore had lost all interest. Sometimes the older women would attend and add a few words from their own experience; or they would suggest, sarcastically, that the Upper House was going the way of the Lower. As for the younger women, either they would not attend at all, or else they came to ask questions, shout denials, groan and hiss, or even pass disagreeable resolutions. Constance knew all this; and though she would have shrunk, almost as much as the Duchess, from lending any aid to revolutionary designs, she could not but feel that the popular sympathy awakened in her favour at such a moment as the present might assume such strength as to be an irresistible force. How could the sympathies of the people be otherwise than on her side? These marriages of old or middle-aged women with young men, common though they had become, could never be regarded by the youth of either sex as natural. The young women bitterly complained that the lovers provided for them by equality of age were taken from them, and that times were so bad that in no profession could one look to marry before forty. The young men, who were not supposed to have any voice in the matter, let it be clearly known that their continual prayer and daily dream was for a young wife. The general discontent found expression in songs and ballads, written no one knew by whom: they passed from hand to hand; they were sung with closed doors; they all had the same motif; they celebrated the loves of two young people, maiden and youth; they showed how they were parted by the elderly woman who came to marry the tall and gallant youth; how the girl's life was embittered, or how she pined away, or how she became misanthropic; and how the young man spent the short remainder of his days in an apathetic endeavour to discharge his duty, fortified on his deathbed with the consolations of religion and the hopes of meeting, not his old wife, but his old love, in a better and happier world. Why, there could be nothing but sympathy with Constance and Lord Chester. Why, all the men, old and young alike, whose influence upon women and popular opinion, though denied by some, was never doubted by Constance, would give her cause their most active sympathies.

She remained at home that day, taking no other step than to charge a friend with the task of communicating the intelligence to her club, being well aware that in an hour or two it would be spread over London, and, in fact, over the whole realm of England. The next day she went down to the House, and had the satisfaction of finding that the excitement caused by her resignation—a ministerial resignation was too common a thing to cause much talk—had given way altogether to the excitement caused by this great Appeal. No one even took the trouble of asking who was going to be the new Home Secretary. It was taken for granted that it would be some friend of the Duchess of Dunstanburgh. The lobbies were crowded—reporters, members of clubs, diners-out, talkers, were hurrying backwards and forwards, trying to pick up a tolerably trustworthy anecdote; and there was the va et vient, the nervous activity, which is so much more easily awakened by personal quarrels than by political differences. And here was a personal quarrel! The young and beautiful Countess against the old and powerful Duchess.

'Yes,' said Constance loudly, in answer to a whispered question put by one of her friends—she may have observed two or three listeners standing about with eager ears and parted lips—'yes, it is all quite true; it was an understood thing—this match with my second cousin. The pretensions of the Duchess rest upon too transparent a foundation—the poor man's money, my dear. As if she were not rich enough already! as if three husbands are not enough for any one woman to lament! Thank you; yes, I have not the slightest doubt of the result. In a matter of good feeling as well as equity one may always depend upon the House, whatever one's political opinions.'

The Duchess certainly had not expected this resistance to her will. In fact, during the whole of her long life she had never known any resistance at all, except such as befalls every politician. But in her private life her will was law, which no one questioned or disputed. Nor did it even occur to her to inquire, before speaking to the Chancellor, whether there would be any rival in the field. Proud as she was, and careless of public opinion in a general way, it was far from pleasant, even for her, to reflect on the things which would be said of her proposal when the Appeal was brought before the House—on the motives which would be assigned or insinuated by her enemies; on the allusions to youth and age—the more keen the more skilfully they were disguised and wrapped in soft words; the open pity which would be expressed for the youth whose young life—she knew very well what would be said—was to be sacrificed; the sarcastic questions which would be asked about the increase of her property by the new marriage, and so forth. The plain speech of Peeresses in debate was well known to her. Yet pride forbade a retreat: she would fight it out; she could command, by ways and by methods only known to herself, a majority; yet she felt sure, beforehand, that it would be a cold and unsympathetic majority—even a reproachful majority. Nor was her temper improved by a visit from her old friend, once her schoolfellow, Lady Despard. She came with a long face, which portended expostulation.

'You have quite made up your mind, Duchess?' she began, without a word of explanation or preamble, but with a comfortable settlement in the chair, which meant a good long talk.

'I have quite made up my mind,' Between such old friends, no need to ask what was intended.

'Lord Chester,' said Lady Despard, thoughtfully, 'who is, no doubt, all that you think him—worthy in every way, I mean, of this promotion and your name—is, after all, a very young man.'

'That,' replied the Duchess spitefully, 'is my affair. His age need not be considered. I am not afraid of myself, Julia. With my experience, at all events, I can say so much.'

'Surely, Duchess; I did not mean that. The most powerful mind, coupled with the highest rank,—how should that fail to attract and fix the affection and gratitude of a man? No, dear friend; what I meant was this: he is too young, perhaps, for the full development either of virtues—or their opposites,—too young, perhaps, to know the reality of the prize you offer him.'

'I think not, Julia,' the Duchess spoke kindly,—'I think not. It is good of you to consider this possibility in so friendly a way; but I have the greatest reliance on the good qualities of Lord Chester. Lady Boltons is his guardian; who would be safer? Professor Ingleby has been his tutor; who could be more discreet?'

'Yes,—Professor Ingleby. She is certainly learned; and yet—yet—at Cambridge there is an uneasy feeling about her orthodoxy.'

'I care little,' said the Duchess, 'about a few wild notions which he may have picked up. On such a man, a little freedom of thought sits gracefully. A Duke of Dunstanburgh cannot possibly be anything but orthodox. Yes, Julia; and the sum of it all is that I am getting old, and I am going to make myself happy with the help of this young gentleman.'

'In that case,' said her friend, 'I have nothing to say, except that I wish you every kind of happiness that you can desire.'

'Thank you, Julia. And you will very greatly oblige me if you will mention, wherever you can, that you know, on the very best authority, that the match will be one of pure affection—on both sides; mind, on both sides.'

'I will certainly say so, if you wish,' replied Lady Despard. 'I think, however, that you ought to know, Duchess, something of what people say—no, not common people, but people whose opinions even you are bound to consider.'

'Go on,' said the Duchess frowning.

'They say that Lord Chester is so proud of his hereditary title and his rank that he would be broken-hearted to see it merged in any higher title; that he is too rich and too highly placed to be tempted by any of the ordinary baits by which men are caught; that you can give him nothing which he cannot buy for himself; and, lastly, that he is already in love,—even that words of affection have been passed between him and the Countess of Carlyon.'

Here the Duchess interrupted, vehemently banging the floor with the crutch which stood at her right hand.

'Lord Chester in love? What nonsense is this, Julia? A young nobleman of his rank—almost my rank—in love! Are you mad, Julia? Are you softening in the brain? Are you aware that the boy has been properly brought up? Will you be good enough to remember that Lady Boltons is beyond all suspicion, and that he could never have seen Lady Carlyon alone since he was a boy?'

'I answer your questions by one or two others,' replied her friend calmly. 'Are you, Duchess, aware that these two young people have had constant opportunities of being alone everywhere—coming from church, going to church, in conservatories, at morning parties, at dances, in gardens? Lady Boltons is all discretion; but still—but still—girls will be girls—boys love to flirt. My dear Duchess, we are still young enough to remember——'

The Duchess smiled: the Duchess laughed. Good humour returned.

'What else, Julia? You are a retailer of horrid gossip.'

'This besides. On the very morning when he waited on the Chancellor, he rode to Lady Carlyon's——'

'I know the exact particulars,' said the Duchess. 'Lady Boltons wrote to me on the subject to prevent misunderstanding. Professor Ingleby, his old tutor, was there. He rode there alone because his guardian could not go with him. Of course he was properly attended. Lady Carlyon is his second cousin. Properly speaking, perhaps he should have remained at home until the Professor came to him. But a man of Lord Chester's rank may do things which smaller men cannot. And, besides, this impulsiveness—this apparent impatience of conventional restraint—seems to me only to prove the pride and dignity of his character. Is that all, Julia? Have you any more hearsays?'

They were brave words; but the Duchess felt uneasy.

'I have; there is more behind, and worse. Still, in your present mood, I do not know that I ought to say what I should wish to say.'

'Say on, Julia. You know that I wish to hear all. Perhaps there may be something after all. Hide nothing from me.'

'Very good. They say that Lord Chester is, of all men, the least submissive, the least docile, the least manly—in the highest sense of the word. He habitually assumes authority which belongs to Us; he flies into violent rages; he horsewhips stable-boys; he presumptuously defies orders; he almost openly derides the laws which regulate man's obedience. He questions—he actually questions—the fundamental principles on which society and government are based.'

'Quite as it should be,' said the Duchess, folding her hands. 'I want my husband to obey no one in the world—except myself: he shall accept no teaching, except mine; no doctrine shall be sacred in his eyes—until it has received my authority.'

'Would you like the Duke of Dunstanburgh to horsewhip stable-boys?'

The Duchess shrugged her shoulders.

'Why not? No doubt the stable-boys deserve it. We cannot, of course, allow common men to use their strength in this way. But, my dear, in men of very high rank we should encourage—within proper limits—a masterfulness which is, after all, nothing but the legitimate expression of legitimate pride. What is crime in a clown or an artisan, is a virtue in Lord Chester; and, believe me, Julia, for my own part, I know how to tame the most obstinate of men.'

She folded her hands and set her teeth together. Julia thought of the late three dukes, and trembled.

'No one should know better, dear Duchess. There remains one thing only. You tell me that the proposed match is to be one of pure affection—on both sides. I am truly rejoiced to hear it. Nothing is better calculated to allay these silly reports about Lady Carlyon and the Earl. Still you should know that outside people say that, should the Appeal go in your favour——'

' "Should!" Julia, do not be absurd. It must go in my favour. "Should!" '

'In that case the Earl has declared before witnesses that he will absolutely refuse, whatever the penalty, to accept your hand. How am I to meet such stories as this? By your authorised statement of mutual affection?'

'Idle gossip, Julia, may be left to itself. The Earl is only anxious to have the matter settled as soon as possible. Besides, is it in reason that he should have made such a declaration? Why, he knows—every man knows—that such a refusal would be nothing short of contempt—contempt of the Sovereign Majesty of the Realm. It is punishable—ay, and it shall be punished—that is, it should be punished'—the face of the Duchess darkened—'by imprisonment with hard labour for life—Earl or no Earl.'

'Then, Duchess,' said Lady Despard, with a smile, 'I say no more. Of course, a marriage of affection should be encouraged; and we women are all match-makers. You will have the best wishes of all as soon as things are properly understood.'

'Julia,' the Duchess laid her hand upon her friend's arm, 'I am unfeignedly glad that you have told me all this. We have had an explanation which has cleared the air. I refuse to believe that my future husband has so lost all manly feeling as to fall in love. Imagine an Earl of Chester falling in love like a sentimental rustic! Your canards about private interviews trouble me not; I am well assured that so well-bred a man will obey the will of the House without a murmur—nay, joyfully, even without consideration of his own inclinations, which, as I have told you, are already decided. And, upon my honour as a peeress, Julia, I am certain that when you come to my autumn party at Dunstanburgh in November next, you will acknowledge that the new Duke is the handsomest bridegroom in the world, that I am the most indulgent wife, and that there is not a happier couple in all England.'

Nothing could be more gracious than the smile of the Duchess when she chose to smile. Lady Despard, although she knew by this time what the smile was worth, was nevertheless always carried away by it. For the moment she believed what her friend wished her to believe.

'My dear Duchess,' she cried with effusion, 'you deserve happiness for your part; and, upon my word, I think that the boy will get it, whether he deserves it or not.'

The smile died out from the Duchess's face when she was left alone. A hard, stern look took its place. She took up a hand-glass, and intently examined her own face.

'He is in love with the girl, is he?' she murmured; 'and she with him. Why, I saw it in their guilty stolen looks; her accents betrayed her when she spoke. It is not enough that she must cross me in the House, but she would rob me of a husband. Not yet, Lady Carlyon—not yet.' ... She looked at herself again. 'Oh, that I could be again what I was at one-and-twenty! It is true, as Julia said, that I have nothing to give the boy in return for what I ask of him—his affection. I am an old woman—sixty-five years of age. I suppose I have had my share of love. Harry loved me when I was young, because I was young. Poor Harry! I did not then know how much he loved me, nor the value of a man's heart. Well ... as for the other two, they loved me after their fashion—but it was not like Harry's love; they said they loved me, and in return I gave them all they wanted. They were happy, and I had to be contented.' She mused in silence for a time; then she roused herself with an effort. 'What then? Let them talk. I am the Duchess of Dunstanburgh. She shall have her whim; she shall have her darling, and if he chooses to sulk, she will punish him until he smiles again. Wait, my lord, only wait till you are safe on the Northumberland coast, and in my castle of Dunstanburgh.'

CHAPTER V. IN THE SEASON

WOMEN, especially politicians, are (or rather were, until the Revolt) accustomed to the publicity of photographs, illustrated papers, paragraphs in society papers, and to the curiosity with which people stare after them wherever they show themselves. They used to like it. Men, who were, on the other hand, taught to respect modest retirement and that graceful obscurity becoming to the masculine hand which carries out the orders of the female brain, shrank from such notoriety. It was a curious sensation for young Lord Chester to feel, rather than to see and to hear, the people pointing him out, and talking about him.

'Courage!' whispered the Professor. 'You will have to encounter a great deal more curiosity than this before long. Above all, do not show by any sign or change of expression that you are conscious of their staring.'

This was at the Royal Academy. The rooms were crowded with the usual mob, for it was early in June. There were the country ladies—rosy, fat, and jolly—catalogue and pencil in hand, dragging after them husbands, brothers, sons—ruddy, stalwart fellows—who wearily followed from room to room,—ignorant of art, and yet unwilling to be thought ignorant,—flocking to any picture which seemed to contain a story or a subject likely to interest them, such as a horse, or a race, or a match of some kind, and turning away with a half-conscious feeling that they ought to rejoice in not liking the much-praised picture, instead of being ashamed of it, so unlike a horse did they find it, so unfaithful a representation of figure or of action. There were artistic ladies with their new fashion of dress and pale languid airs, listlessly exchanging the commonplace of the fashionable school; there were professional ladies, lawyers, and doctors, 'doing' all the rooms between two consultations in an hour; there were schoolgirls from Harrow, yawning over the Exhibition, which it was a duty they owed to themselves to see early in the season, unless they could get tickets, which they all ardently desired, for the fortnight's private view; there were shoals of men in little parties of two and four, escorted by some good-natured uncle or elderly cousin. The crowd squeezed round the fashionable pictures; they passed heedlessly before pictures of which nobody talked; they all tried to look critical; those who pretended to culture searched after strange adjectives; those who did not, said everything was pretty, and yawned furtively; the ladies whispered remarks to each other, with a quick nod of intelligence; and they received the feeble criticism of the men with the deferent smile due to politeness, or a half-concealed contempt.

This year there were more than the usual number of pictures—in fact, the whole of the five-and-twenty rooms were crowded. Fortunately, they were mostly small rooms, and it was remarkable that the same subjects occurred over and over again. 'The same story,' said the Professor, 'every year. No invention; we follow like sheep. Here is Judith slaying Holofernes'—they were then in the Ancient History Department—'here is Jael slaying Sisera; here are Miriam and Deborah singing their songs of triumph; here is Joan of Arc raising the siege of Orleans,—all exactly the same as when I was a girl forty years ago and more. Ancient History, indeed! What do they know about Ancient History?'

'Why do you not teach them, then, Professor?' asked Lord Chester.

'I will tell you why, my lord, in a few weeks,—perhaps.'

There were a great many altar-pieces in the Sacred Department. In these the Perfect Woman was depicted in every attitude and occupation by which perfection may best be represented. It might have been objected, had any one so far ventured outside the beaten path of criticism, that the Perfect Woman's dress, her mode of dressing her hair, and her ornaments were all of the present year's fashion. 'As if,' said the Professor, the only one who did venture, 'as if no one had any conception of beauty and grace except what fashion orders. Sheep! sheep! we follow like a flock.'

The pictures were mostly allegorical: the Perfect Woman directed Labour—represented by twenty or thirty burly young men with implements of various kinds; this was a very favourite subject. Or she led Man upwards. This was a series of pictures: in the first, Man was a rough rude creature, carrying a club with which he banged something—presumably Brother Man; he gradually improved, until at the end he was depicted as laying at the altar of womanhood flowers, fruit, and wine, from his own husbandry. By this time he had got his beard cut off, and was smooth shaven, save for a pair of curly moustaches; his dress was in the fashion of the day; his eyes were down-dropped in reverential awe; and his expression was delightfully submissive, pious, and béate. 'Is it,' asked Lord Chester, 'impossible to be religious without becoming such a creature as that?'

Again, the Perfect Woman sat alone, thinking for the good of the world. She had a star above her head; she tried, in the picture, not to look as if she were proud of that star. Or the Perfect Woman sat watching, in the dead of night, in the moonlight, for the good of the world; or the Perfect Woman was revealed to enraptured man rising from the waves, not at all wet, and clothed in the most beautifully-fashioned and most expensive modern garments. These two rooms, the Sacred and the Ancient History Departments, were mostly deserted. The principal interest of the Exhibition was in the remaining three-and-twenty, which were devoted to general subjects. Here were sweetnesses of flower and fruit, here were lovely creamy faces of male youth, here were full length figures of athletes, runners, wrestlers, jumpers, rowers, cricket-players, and others, treated with delicate conventionality, so that the most successful pictures represented man with no more expression in his face than a barber's block, and the strongest young Hercules was figured with tiny hands or fingers like a girl's for slimness, for transparency, and for whiteness, and beautifully small feet; on the other hand, his calves were prodigious. In fact, as was always maintained at the Academy dinner, the Exhibition was the great educator of the people in the sense of beauty. To know the beautiful, to recognise what should be delightful, and then take joy in it, was given, it was said, only to those women of culture who had been trained by a course of Academy exhibitions. Here men, for their part, who would never otherwise rise beyond the phenomenal to the ideal, learned what was the Perfect Man—the Man of woman's imagination. Having learned, he might go away and try to resemble him. Women who could not feel, unhappily, the full sense of the beautiful, might learn from these models into what kind of man they should shape their husbands.

'The drawing of this picture,' said the Professor aloud, before a picture round which were gathered a throng of worshippers—for it was painted by a Royal Academician of great repute—'is inaccurate. Did one ever see a man with such shoulders, and yet with such a waist and such a hand? As for the colouring, it is as false as it is conventional; and look at the peach-like cheek and the feeble chin! It is the flesh of a weakly baby, not of a grown man and an athlete.'

There were murmurs of dissent, but no one ventured to dispute the Professor's opinion; and indeed most of the bystanders had already recognised Lord Chester, and were staring at the hero of so much talk.

'He is better-looking,' he overheard one schoolgirl whispering to another, 'than the fellow on the canvas, isn't he?'

The 'fellow on the canvas' was, in fact, the Ideal Man. He was meant by the artist to represent the noblest, tallest, strongest, straightest, and most dexterous of men. He carried a cricket-bat. It would have been foolish to figure him with book, pencil, or paper. Art, literature, science, politics, all belonged to the other sex. Only his strength was left to man, and that was to be expended by the orders of the superior sex, who were quite competent to exercise the functions for which they were born—namely, to think for the world.

Of course, all the artists were women. Once there was a man who, assuming a female name, actually got a picture exhibited in the Academy. He was a self-taught man it was afterwards discovered; he had never been in a studio; he had never seen a Royal Academy. He painted an Old Man from nature. There was a faithful ruggedness about his work which made artists scoff, and yet brought tears to the eyes of country girls who knew no better. When the trick was discovered, the picture was taken down and burnt, and the wretched man—who was discovered in a little country cottage, painting two or three more in the same style—went mad, and was locked up for the rest of his days. Presently Lord Chester grew tired of the pictures and of the staring crowd. 'I have seen enough, Professor, if you have. They are all exactly like those of last year—the gladiators, and the runners, and all. Are we always to go on producing the same pictures?'

'I suppose so,' she replied. 'They say that the highest point of art has been reached. It would be a change if we were only to deteriorate for a few years. Meanwhile, one is reminded of the mole, who was asked why he did not invent another form of architecture.'

'What did she reply?'

'He, not she, my lord, replied that science could go no further; and so he goes on building the same shaped hill.'

The crowd gathered at the foot of the stairs of the Academy and made a lane for Lord Chester quite to his carriage. It was a crowd of the best people in England, composed of ladies and gentlemen. Yet was it no insignificant sign of the times that many a handkerchief was waved to him, that all hats were lifted, and that one girl's voice was heard crying, 'Young men for young wives!' at which there was a general murmur of assent.

In the evening there were the usual engagements of the season, beginning with a lecture on the Arrival at the Highest Level. The lecturer—a young Oxford woman—was learned and eloquent, though the subject was, so to speak, wellnigh threadbare. Yet the discontent of the nation was so great, that it was necessary continually to raise the courage of the people by showing that if the Ministries failed, it was only because the right Cabinet had not yet been found. On this night, however, no one listened. All eyes were turned to the young lord, who, it was everywhere stated, had announced his rebellious intention not to obey the law if Lady Carlyon's appeal went against her. The men whispered; the elderly ladies assumed airs of virtuous indignation; the younger ones looked at each other and laughed.

Then there was a dance, at which Lord Chester was seen, but only for a quarter of an hour, because the rush made by all the girls who could get an introduction for his name on their cards was almost unseemly. The Professor therefore took him home.

In the Park the next afternoon, at the theatre in the evening, the same curiosity of the multitude. Indeed the play, as happened very often in those days, was entirely neglected. Glasses were levelled at Lord Chester's box; the whole audience with one consent fell to talking among themselves; the actors went on with the piece unregarded, and the curtain fell unnoticed.

Perhaps the perfection of the drama was the thing on which the new civilisation chiefly prided itself, unless, indeed, it was the perfection of painting and sculpture already described. The old tragedies, in which women played the secondary part, were long since consigned to oblivion. The old style of farce, which was simply brutal, raising laughter by the representation of situations in which one or more persons are made ridiculous, was absolutely prohibited; the once favourite ballet was suppressed, because it was below the dignity of woman to dance for the amusement of the people, and because neither men nor women wished to see men dancing; the comic man naturally disappeared with the farce, because no one ever wrote anything for him. It was resolved, after a series of letters and discussion in the Academy, the only literary paper left—it owed its continued existence to the honourable associations of its early years—that laughter was for the most part vulgar; that it always rudely disturbed the facial lines; that to make merriment for others was quite beneath the notice of an educated woman; and that the drama must be severe, and even austere—a school for women and for men. Such it was sought to make it, with as yet unsatisfactory results, because the common people, finding nothing to laugh at, came no more to the theatre; and even the better class, who wanted to be amused, and were only instructed, ceased to attend.

When, therefore, the curtain fell, the scanty audience rushed to the doors of the house, and there was something very much like a demonstration, a report of which, the Professor felt with pleasurable emotion, could not fail to be carried to the Duchess.

The next day there came a letter to Lady Boltons—who was still confined to her room with gout—from no less a person than the Duchess of Dunstanburgh, suggesting that the publicity thrust upon Lord Chester through the unconstitutional action of his cousin might produce an injurious effect upon a mind so young. In other words, her Grace was already sensible of the sympathy which was growing up for what was believed to be a love affair, cruelly blighted by herself. If Lord Chester was kept in retirement until the case was decided, he would, perhaps be forgotten. As for Lady Carlyon, the Duchess rightly judged that the sympathy which one woman gets from another in such cases is generally scant.

No doubt she was right, but unfortunately she was too late. The young Earl had been seen everywhere; his story, much altered and improved, was in everybody's mouth; his likeness was in all the shop windows, side by side with that of Lady Carlyon, or, as if to give emphasis to the difference between the two suitors, he was placed with the Duchess on his left and Lady Carlyon on his right. The young men envied him because he was so rich, so handsome, and so gallant; the young ladies looked and sighed. He was nearer the Ideal Man than any they had ever seen; his bold and daring eyes struck them with a kind of awe, which they thought was due to his rank, ignorant of the manhood in those eyes, which attracted and yet daunted them. They bought his photograph by thousands, and spent their leisure hours, or even the hours of study, when they ought to have been 'mugging bones,' or drawing contracts, or reading theology, in gazing upon that remarkable presence. Older ladies—those who had established positions and could think of marriage—wished that such young men were within their reach; and very old ladies, looking at the photograph with admiring eyes, would wag their heads, and tell their grandsons how their grandfather, dead and gone, had been just such another as Lord Chester—so handsome, so strong, so brave, and yet withal the most dutiful and obedient of husbands. They did not explain how the virtue of submission was compatible with such frank and fearless eyes.

The mischief, therefore, was done. So far as the sympathies of the people were concerned, Constance could rest content. There remained, however, the House.

Lord Chester appeared no more in public. He went to none of the cricket-matches and athletics which made the season so lively; nor was he seen at any balls or dinners; nor did he ride in the Row. He was kept in almost monastic seclusion, a few companions only being invited to play tennis on his own lawns. But the Professor was with him constantly—Lady Boltons continuing to be laid up with her gout—and they had long talks in the gardens, sitting beneath the shade of the trees, or walking on the lawns. During these conversations the young man would clench his fist and stamp his foot with rage; or his eyes would kindle, and he would stretch out his right hand as if moved beyond control. And he became daily more masterful, insomuch that the women were afraid of him, and the men-servants—whom he had cuffed until they respected him—laughed, seeing the dismay of the women. Never any man like him! 'Why,' said the butler, a most respectable old lady, 'if he goes on like this, he'll be like the Duchess of Dunstanburgh herself. She'll have a handful, whichever o' their ladyships gets him. Beer, my lord? At twelve o'clock in the morning! It isn't good for your lordship. Better wait—oh dear, dear! Yes, my lord, in one minute.'

One afternoon, towards the end of June, a little party had been made up for his amusement. It consisted of half a dozen young men of his own age, and a few ladies whose age more nearly approached that of the Professor. The young men played one or two matches of tennis, changed their flannels for morning dress, and joined the ladies at afternoon tea. The one topic of conversation possible at the moment was forbidden in that house: it was, of course, that of the great Appeal, and how some said that the Countess wanted it pushed on, so as to take advantage of the public sympathy, and the Duchess wanted it delayed, so as to give this feeling time to cool down; but the Duchess had sworn by everything dear to her that she would marry the young lord whether the House gave a decision in her favour or not; how Lady Carlyon declared that she would carry him off under the very nose of the Duchess; with a thousand other canards, rumours, little secrets, whispers on the best authority, and so forth. As, of course, that could not be entered upon in Lord Chester's own house, the afternoon was dull to the ladies. They pumped the Professor artfully, but learned nothing. She was enthusiastic in her praises of her pupil, but was reticent about his previous relations, if any, with either of his suitors; nor would she reveal anything, if she knew anything, about his inclinations—if he had any preference. As for his character, she spoke openly; he was certainly,—well, say masterful—that could not be denied—in a way which would be unbecoming in a man below his rank; as for his religion, no one could more truly love and revere the Perfect Woman than did Lord Chester; as for his abilities, they were far beyond the common: and for his reading, 'I have always considered,' said the Professor, 'his rank as of more importance than his sex; and though I have, perhaps, given him a wider and deeper education than is generally considered prudent for the masculine brain, I believe it will be found, in the long-run, a course productive of great good. In fact,' she whispered, 'I believe that Lord Chester is a man likely to be the father of daughters, illustrious not only by their birth, but also by their strength of intellect and force of character.'

'No man,' said one of the guests—one of those persons who always know how to find the right commonplace at the right time,—'no man can have a more worthy object of ambition. To sink himself in the family, to work for them, to reproduce his own virtues in their higher feminine form in his own daughters,—I hope his lordship will obtain this happiness.'

'But he can't,' cried another—one of those persons who always say the wrong things,—'he can't if he marries the Duc—'

'Hush!' said the Professor. 'My dear madam, we were talking, I think, about Lord Chester's character. Yes, he is in many respects a most remarkable young man.'

'But is he,' asked another lady, 'is he quite—are you sure of what you say, Professor, about his orthodoxy?'

Professor Ingleby smiled. All smiled, indeed, because her own faith had been greatly suspected, as everybody knew.

'As sure,' she said, 'as I am of my own. Oh! I know what wicked people have hinted at Cambridge. But wait; have patience; I will before long prove my religious convictions, and satisfy the world once for all, in a way that will perhaps astonish, but certainly convince everybody, what my faith really is, and how truly orthodox—and I will answer for my pupil.'

Then the young men appeared, and they began to talk about the games over their tea. Presently they pressed Lord Chester to sing. No one had a better voice, or sang with greater expression. He refused at first, on the ground of being tired of the words of all his songs, but gave way and sang, with a laughing protest at the sentiment of the song and the inanity of the words, the following ballad, just then popular:—

'Through sweet buttercups, through sweet hay
Rolled in swathes by the southern wind;
Side by side they wended their way;
The sloping sun on their faces lay,
And dragged long shadows behind.

'Eighteen he, and stalwart to see;
Muscles of steel and a heart of gold.
Cheeks hot-burning, and eyes down-dropped,—
What did he think when she suddenly stopped,
And gave him her hand—to hold?

'She was but thirty; her lands around
Lay with orchards and cornfields spread;

Meadow and hill with the sunlight crowned,
Wealth and joy without stint or bound,
And all for the lad she would wed!
'He listened in silence, as young men should,
While she pictured the life to come;
In tangled copse, in the way of the wood,
With new spring flowers and old leaves strewed,
She spoke of a love-lit home.
'Only a year: and the hay again
Lies in swathes, like the weed on the shore;
Lone he wanders with troubled brain,
Crying, "When will she come again?"
Poor fool; for she comes no more.
Forgotten her troth; and broken her oath;
His love will return no more.
'The air is not bad,' said the singer, when he had finished, rising from the piano,' but the words are ridiculous. As if he were likely to care for a woman eighteen years his senior!'
These words fell among them like a bomb. There was a dead silence. No one dared raise her eyes except the Professor, who looked up in warning.
Presently an old gentleman, who had been half asleep, shook his head and spoke.
'The songs are all alike now. A young fellow gets made love to, and is engaged, and then thrown over. Then he breaks his heart: In real life he would have called for his horse and galloped off his disappointment.'
'Come, Sir George,' said the Professor, 'you must allow us a little sentiment—some belief in man's heart, else life would be too dull. For my own part, I find the words touching and true to nature.'
'How would it do?' asked Lord Chester, smiling, 'to invert the thing? Could we have a ballad showing how a young lady—she must be young—pined away and died for love of a man who broke his promise?'
They all laughed at this picture, but the young men looked as if Lord Chester had said something wonderful in its audacity. Most certainly, thought the Professor, his words would be quoted in all the clubs that very day. And what—oh! what would the Duchess say? And although she had no legitimate power over the ward of Chancery, she could do what she pleased with the Chancellor.
There was one young fellow present, a certain Algy Dunquerque, who entertained an affection for Lord Chester amounting almost to worship. No one was like him; none so strong, so dexterous, so good at games; no one so clever; no one so audacious; no one so gloriously independent.
They were talking together in a low whisper, unregarded by the ladies, who were talking loudly.
'Algy,' said Lord Chester, 'you said once that you would come to me if ever I asked you, and stand by me as long as I asked you. Are you still of the same mind?'
'That kind of promise holds,' said Algy. 'What shall I do?'
'Be in readiness.'
'I am always ready. But what are you going to do? Shall we run away together?'
'Hush! I do not know,—yet. All that a desperate man can do.'

CHAPTER VI. WOMAN'S ENGLAND

THE next day was Sunday, and of course Lord Chester went to church with the Professor, who was always careful to observe forms.

The congregation was large, and principally composed of men. The service was elaborate, and the singing good. Perhaps the incense was a little too strong, and there was some physical fatigue in the frequent changes of posture. Nothing, however, could have been more splendid than the procession with banners, which closed the service; nothing sweeter than the voices of the white-robed singing-girls. It was a large and beautiful church, with painted glass, pictures having lights burning before them; and the altar, on which stood the veiled figure of the Perfect Woman, was heaped with flowers.

The sermon was preached by the Dean of Westminster, whose eloquence and fervour were equalled by her scholarship. No one, except perhaps, Professor Ingleby, was better read in ecclesiastical history, or knew more about the beginnings of the New Religion. She had written a book, showing from ancient literature how the germs of the religion were dormant even in the old barbaric times of man's supremacy. Even so far back as the Middle Ages men delighted to honour Woman. Every poet chose a mistress for his devotion, and ignorantly worshipped the type in the Individual. Every knight became servant and slave to one woman, in whose honour his noblest deeds were done. Even the worship of the Divine Man became, first in Catholic countries, and afterwards in England, through a successful conspiracy of certain so-called 'ritualists,' the worship of the Mother and Child. At all times the effigies of the virtues, Faith, Hope, Love, had been figures of women. The form of woman had always stood for the type, the standard, the ideal of the Beautiful. The woman had always been the dispenser of gifts. The woman had always been richly dressed. Men worked their hardest in order to pour their treasures into the lap of woman. All the reverence, all the poetry, all the imagination with which the lower nature of man was endowed, had been freely spent and lavished in the service of woman. From his earliest infancy, women surrounded, protected, and thought for men. Why, what was this, what could this mean, but a foreshadowing, an indication, a revelation, by slow and natural means, of the worship of the Perfect Woman, dimly comprehended as yet, but manifesting its power over the heart? The Dean handled this, her favourite topic, in the pulpit this morning with singular force and eloquence. After touching on the invisible growth of the religion, she painted a time of anarchy, when men had given up their old beliefs and were like children—only children with weapons in their hands—crying out with fear in the darkness. She told how women, at last assuming their true place, substituted, little by little, the true, the only faith—the Worship of the Perfect Woman, the Feminine Divinity of Thought, Purpose, and Production. She pointed out how, by natural religion, man was evidently marked out for the second or lower creature, although, by the abuse of his superior strength, he had wrested the authority and used it for his own purposes. He was formed to execute, he was strong, he was the Agent. Woman, on the other hand, was the mother—that is to say, the Creative Thought; that is, the Sovereign Ruler. In the animal creation, again, it is the male who works, while the female sits and directs. And even in such small points as the gender of things inanimate, everything of grace, usefulness, or beauty was, and always had been, feminine. Then she argued from the natural quickness and intelligence of women, and from the corresponding dullness of men, from the lower instincts of men compared with the spiritual nature of women; and she showed how, when women took their natural place in the government of the nation, laws were for the first time framed on sound and economical principles, and for the benefit of man himself. Finally, in a brilliant peroration, she called upon her male hearers to defend, even to the death if necessary, the principles of their religion; she warned the women that a spirit of questioning and discontent was abroad; she exhorted the men to find their true happiness in submission to authority; and she drew a vivid picture of the poor wretch who, beginning with doubt and disobedience, went on to wife-beating, atheism, and despair, both of this world and the next.

The sermon lasted nearly an hour. The Dean never paused, never hesitated, was never at a loss. Yet, somehow she failed to affect her hearers. The women looked idly about them, the men stared straight before them, showing no response, and no sympathy. One reason of this apathy was that the congregation had heard it all before, and so often, that it ceased to move them; the priestesses of the Faith, in their ardour, endeavouring constantly to make men intelligent as well as submissive supporters, overdid the preaching, and by continual repetition ruined the effect of their earnest eloquence, and reduced it to the level of rhetorical commonplace.

The Professor and her pupil walked gravely homewards.

'I think,' said Lord Chester, 'that I could preach a sermon the other way round.'

'You mean——'

'I mean that I could just as well show how natural religion intended man to be both agent and contriver.'

'I think,' said the Professor, 'that such a sermon had better not be preached, at least, just yet. It was rather a risky thing to make that remark of yours about the ballad which you sang yesterday. Such a sermon as you contemplate would infallibly land its composer—even Lord Chester—in a prison—and for life.'

Lord Chester was silent.

'Do you speculate often,' asked his tutor, 'in these theological matters?'

'Of late,' he replied. 'Yes, this perpetual admonition about Authority worries me. Why should we accept statements on Authority? I have been looking through the text-books, and I conclude——'

'Pray do not tell me,' she interrupted laughing. 'For the present, let me not know the nature of your conclusions. But, Lord Chester, for your own sake, for every one's sake, be guarded—be silent,' She pressed his arm; he nodded gravely, but made no reply. When they reached home they learned that the Chancellor herself was waiting to see Lord Chester. She wished to see the Professor as well.

The Chancellor was in a great worry and fidget—as if this unhappy business of the Appeal was not enough for her—because, whatever decision was arrived at by the House, she would have to defend her own, and there was little doubt that her enemies would not lose so good a chance of attacking her; and now the boy must needs get saying things which were repeated in every club in London.

'I must say, Lord Chester,' she began irritably, 'that a little respect—I say a little respect—is due to a person who holds my office. I have been waiting for you a good quarter of an hour.'

'Had I known your ladyship's wish to see me, I would have saved you the trouble of coming here, and waited upon you myself. I have but just returned from church.' 'Church!' she repeated in mockery; 'what is the good of people going to church if they fly in the face of all religion? Do not answer me, pray. Your lordship thinks yourself, I know, a privileged person. You are to say, and to do, anything you please. But I am the Chancellor, remember, and your guardian. Now, sir, I learn that you make dangerous, revolutionary remarks—you made one yesterday—openly, on the impossibility of a young man marrying a woman older than himself.'

'Pardon me,' said Lord Chester; 'I did not say the impossibility of marrying, but of loving, a woman twenty years his senior.'

'The distinction shows the unhappy condition of your mind. To marry a woman is to love her.

What would the boy want? what would he have? Professor Ingleby, have you anything to advise? He is your pupil. You are, in fact, partly responsible for this deplorable exhibition of wilfulness.'

'With your ladyship's permission,' replied the Professor softly, 'I would venture to suggest that, considering recent events, it would be much better for Lord Chester to be out of London as soon as possible.'

'What is the use of talking about leaving town when Lady Boltons is ill?'

'If your ladyship will entrust your noble ward to my care,' continued the Professor, 'I will undertake the charge of him at my own house for the next three months.'

The Chancellor reflected. The plan seemed the best. Since Lady Boltons was ill, there was really no one to look after the young man, while, at the present moment of excitement, it seemed most desirable that he should be out of town. If the boy was to go on talking in this way about old women and young men, there was no telling what might not happen; and the Duchess would be pleased with such an arrangement. That consideration decided her.

'If you really can take charge of him—you could draw on Lady Boltons for whatever you like, in reason,—it does seem the best thing to do. Yes—he would be safer out of the way. When can you start?'

'To-morrow.'

'Very good; then we will settle it so. You will accompany Professor Ingleby, Lord Chester; you will consider her as your guardian—and—and all that. And for Heaven's sake, let us have no more folly!'

She touched his fingers with her own, bowed slightly to the Professor, and left them.

'My dear boy,' said the Professor, when the door was shut, 'I foresee a great opportunity. And as for that sermon you spoke of——'

'Well, Professor?'

'You may begin to compose it as soon as you please, and on the road I will help you. Meantime, hold your tongue.'

With these enigmatic words the Professor left him.

There was really nothing very remarkable in Lord Chester's leaving London even at the height of the season. Most of the athletic meetings were over; it was better to be in the country than in town: a young man of two-and-twenty is not supposed to take a very keen delight in dinner-parties. Had it not been for the Appeal and the way in which people occupied themselves in every kind of gossip over Lord Chester—what he said, how he looked, and what he hoped—he might have left town without the least notice being taken. As it was, his departure gave rise to the wildest rumours, not the least wild being that the Duchess, or, as some said, the Countess, intended to follow and carry him off from his country house.

Without troubling themselves about rumours and alarms of this kind, the Professor and her pupil drove away in the forenoon of Monday. The air was clear and cool; there was a fresh breeze, a warm sun, and a sky flecked with light clouds. The leaves on the trees were at their best, the four horses were in excellent condition. What young fellow of two-and-twenty would have felt otherwise than happy at starting on a holiday away from the restraints of town, and in such weather?

'There is only one thing wanting,' he said, as they finally cleared the houses, and were bowling along the smooth highroad between hedges bright with the flowers of early summer.

'What is that?' asked the Professor.

'Constance,' he replied boldly; 'she ought to be with us to complete my happiness.'

The Professor laughed.

'A most unmanly remark,' she said. 'How can you reconcile it with the precepts of morality? Have you not been taught the wickedness of expressing, even of allowing yourself to feel an inclination for any young lady?'

'It is your fault, my dear Professor. You have taught me so much, that I have left off thinking of unmanliness and immodesty and the copy-book texts.'

'I have taught you,' she replied gravely, 'things enough to hang myself and send you to the Tower for life. But remember—remember—that you have been taught these things with a purpose.'

'What purpose?' he asked.

'I began by making you discontented. I allowed you to discover that everything is not so certain as boys are taught to believe. I put you in the way of reading, and I opened your mind to all sorts of subjects generally concealed from young men.'

'You certainly did, and you are a most crafty as well as a most beneficent Professor.'

'You have gradually come to understand that your own intellect, the average intellect of Man, is really equal to the consideration of all questions, even those generally reserved and set apart for women.'

'Is it not time, therefore, to let me know this mysterious purpose?'

Professor Ingleby gazed upon him in silence for a while.

'The purpose is not mine. It is that of a wiser and greater being than myself, whose will I carry out and whom I obey.'

'Wiser than you, Professor? Who is she? Do you mean the Perfect Woman herself?'

'No,' she replied; 'the being whom I obey and reverence is none other than—my own husband.'

Lord Chester started.

'Your husband?' he cried. 'You obey your husband? This is most wonderful.'

'My husband. Yes, Lord Chester, you may now compose that sermon which shall show how Man is the Lord and Master of all created things, including—Woman. I told you I would help you in your sermon. Listen.'

All that day they drove through the fair garden, which we call England. Along the road they passed the rustics hay-making in the fields; the country women were talking at their doors; the country doctor was plodding along her daily round; the parson was jogging along the wayside, umbrella in hand, to call upon her old people; the country police in blue bonnets, carrying their dreaded pocket-books, were loitering in couples about cross-roads; the farmer drove her cart to market, or rode her cob about the fields; little girls and boys carried dinner to their fathers. Here and there they passed a country-seat, a village with its street of cottages, or they clattered through a small sleepy town with its row of villas and its quiet streets, where the men sat working at the windows in hopes of getting a chat or seeing something to break the monotony of the day.

The travellers saw, but noted nothing. For the Professor was teaching her pupil things calculated to startle even the Duchess, and at which Constance would have trembled—things which made his cheek to glow, his eyes to glisten, his mouth to quiver, his hands to clench;—things not to be spoken, not to be whispered, not to be thought, this Professor openly, boldly, and without shame, told the young man.

'I might have guessed it,' he said. 'I had already half guessed it. And this—this is the reason why we are kept in subjection!—this is the LIE they have palmed upon us!'

'Hush! calm yourself. The thing was not done in a day. The system was not invented by conscious hypocrites and deceivers; it grew, and with it the new religion, the new morality, the new order of things. Blame no one, Lord Chester, but blame the system.'

'You have told me too much now,' he said; 'tell me more.'

She went on. Each word, each new fact, tore something from him that he would have believed part of his nature. Yet he had been prepared for this day by years of training, all designed by this crafty woman to arm him with strength to receive her disclosures.

'What you see,' she said, as they drove through a village, 'seems calm and happy. It is the calmness of repression. Those men in the fields, those working men sitting at the windows—they are all alike unhappy, and they know not why. It is because the natural order has been reversed; the sex which should command and create is compelled to work in blind obedience. You will see, as we go on, that we, who have usurped the power, have created nothing, improved nothing, carried on nothing. It is for you, Lord Chester, to restore the old order.'

'If I can—if I can find words,' he stammered.

'I have trusted you,' the Professor went on, 'from the very first. Bon sang ne peut mentir. Yet it was wise not to hurry matters. Your life, and my own life too, if that matters much, hang upon the success of my design. Nothing could have happened more opportunely than the Duchess's proposal. Why? on the one hand, a sweet, charming, delightful girl; and on the other, a repulsive, bad-tempered old woman. While your blood is aflame with love and disgust, Lord Chester, I tell you this great secret. We have three months before us. We must use it, so that in less than two we shall be able to strike, and to strike hard. You are in my hands. We have, first, much to see and to learn.'

Their first halt was Windsor. Here, after ordering dinner, the Professor took her pupil to visit Eton. It was half-holiday, and the girls were out of school. Some were at the Debating Society's rooms, where a political discussion was going on; some were strolling by the river under the grand old elms; some were reading novels in the shade; some were lying on the bank talking and laughing. It was a pleasant picture of happy school life.

'Look at these buildings,' said the Professor, taking up a position of vantage. 'They were built by one of your ancestors, beautified by another, repaired and enlarged by another. This is the noblest of the old endowments—for boys.'

The Earl looked round him in wonder.

'What would boys do with such a splendid place?' he asked.

'Have my lessons borne so little fruit that you should ask that question?' The Professor looked disappointed. 'My dear boy, they played in the playing-fields, they swam and rowed in the river, they studied in the school, they worshipped in the chapel. When it was resolved to divide the endowments, women naturally got the first choice, and they chose Eton. Afterwards the boys' public schools fell gradually into decay, and bit by bit they were either closed or became appropriated by girls. There was once a famous school at a place called Rugby. That died. The Lady of the Manor, I believe, gradually absorbed the revenues. Harrow and Marlborough fell in, after a few years, for girls. You see, when once mothers realised the dangers of public school life for boys, they naturally left off sending them.'

'Yes—I see—the danger that——'

'That they would become masterful, Lord Chester, like yourself; that they would use their strength to recover their old supremacy; that they would discover'—here she sank her voice, although they were not within earshot of any one—'that they would discover how strength of brain goes with strength of muscle.'

She led the young man back across the river to the Windsor side. On the way they passed an open gate; over the gate was written 'Select school for young gentlemen.' Within was a gymnasium, where a dozen boys were exercising on parallel bars swinging with ropes, and playing with clubs.

'As for your education,' said the Professor, 'we have discovered that the best chance for the world is for a boy to be taught three things. He must learn religion—i.e. submission, and the culture of Perfect Womanhood; he must learn a trade of some kind, unless he belongs to the aristocracy, so as not to be necessarily dependent; and he must be made healthy, strong, and active. History will credit us with one thing, at least; we have improved the race.'

It wanted an hour of dinner. The Professor, who was never tired, led her pupil over such portions of the old Castle as could still be visited—the great tower and one or two of the terraces.

'This was once yours,' she said. 'This is the castle of your ancestors. Courage, my lord; you shall win it back.'

It was in a dream that the young man spent the rest of the evening. The Professor had ordered a simple yet dainty dinner, consisting of a Thames trout, a Châteaubriand, quails, and an omelette, with some Camembert cheese, but her young charge did scanty justice to it. After dinner, when the coffee had been brought, and the door was safely shut, the Professor continued the course of lectures on ancient history, by which she had already upset the mind of her pupil, and filled his brain with dreams of a revolution more stupendous than was ever suspected by the watchful bureau of police.

Their next day's drive brought them to Oxford. It was vacation, and the colleges were empty. Only here and there a solitary figure of some lonely Fellow or Lecturer, lingering after the rest had gone, flitted across the lawns. The solitude of the place pleased the Professor. She could ramble with her pupil about the venerable courts and talk at her ease.

'Here,' she said, 'in the old days was once the seat of learning and wisdom.'

'What is it now?' asked her disciple, surprised. 'Is not Oxford still the seat of learning?'

'You must read—alas! you would not understand them—the old books before you can answer your own question. What is their political economy, their moral philosophy, their social science—of which they make so great a boast—compared with the noble scholarship, the science, the speculation of former days? How can I make you understand? There was a time when everything was advanced—by men. Science must advance or fall back. We took from men their education, and science has been forgotten. We cannot now read the old books; we do not understand the old discoveries; we cannot use the tools which they invented, the men of old. Mathematics, chemistry, physical science, geology—all these exist no longer, or else exist in such an elementary form as our ancestors would have been ashamed to acknowledge. Astronomy, which widened the heart, is neglected; medicine has become a thing of books; mechanics are forgotten——'

'But why?'

'Because women, who can receive, cannot create; because at no time has any woman enriched the world with a new idea, a new truth, a new discovery, a new invention; because we have undertaken the impossible.'

The Professor was silent. Never before had Lord Chester seen her so deeply moved.

'Oh, Sacred Learning!' she cried, 'we have sinned against thee! We poor women in our conceit think that everything may be learned from books: we worship the Ideal Woman, and we are content with the rags of learning which remain from the work of Man. Yes, we are contented with these scraps. We will accept nothing that is not absolutely certain. Therefore we blasphemously and ignorantly say that the last word has been said upon everything, and that no more remains to be learned.'

'Mankind is surrounded,' the Professor went on as if talking to herself, 'by a high wall of black ignorance and mystery. The wall is for ever receding or closing in upon us. The men of the past pushed it back more and more, and widened continually the boundaries of thought, so that the foremost among them were godlike for knowledge and for a love of knowledge. We women of the present are continually contracting the wall, so that soon we shall know nothing, unless—unless you come to our help.'

'How can I help to restore knowledge,' asked the young man, 'being myself so ignorant?'

'By giving back the university to the sex which can enlarge our bounds.'

Always the same thing—always coming back to the one subject.

There was a university sermon in the afternoon, being the feast of St Cecilia; they looked in, but the church was empty. In vacation time one hardly expects more than two or three resident lecturers with their husbands and boys, and a sprinkling of young men from the town. The sermon was dull—perhaps Lord Chester's mind was out of sympathy with the subject; it treated on the old well-worn lines of Woman as the Musician.

'I will show you at Cambridge,' said the Professor when they came out, 'some of the music of the past. What are the feeble strains, the oft-repeated phrases of modern music, compared with the grand old music conceived and written by men? Women have never composed great music.'

They left Oxford the next day and proceeded north.

'I think,' said the Professor as they were driving smoothly along the road, 'that they did wrong in not trying to maintain the old railways. True there were many accidents, and sometimes great loss of life; yet it must have been a convenience to get from London to Liverpool in five hours. To be sure the art of making engines is dead: such arts could not survive when their new system of separate labour was introduced.'

They passed the old tracks of the railways from time to time, now long canals grass-grown, and now high embankments covered with trees and bushes. There were black holes, too, in the hill-sides through which the iron road had once run.

'The country in the nineteenth century,' said the Professor, 'was populous and wealthy; but it would be at first terrible for one of us to see and to live in. From end to end there were great factories driven by steam-engines, in which men worked in gangs, and from which a perpetual black cloud of smoke rose to the sky; trains ran shrieking along the iron roads with more clouds of smoke and steam. The results of the work were grand; but the workmen were uncared for, and killed by the long hours and the foul atmosphere. I talk like a woman'—she checked herself with a smile,—'and I want to talk so that you shall feel like a man—of the ancient type.'

'There is one point of difference between man's and woman's legislation which I would have you bear in mind. Man looks to the end, woman thinks of the means. If man wanted a great thing done, he cared little about the sufferings of those who did that thing. A great railway had to be built; those who made it perished of fever and exposure. What matter? The railway remained. A great injustice had to be removed; to remove it cost a war, with death to thousands. Man cared little for the deaths, but much for the result. Man was like Nature, which takes infinite pains to construct an insect of marvellous beauty, and then allows it to be crushed in thousands almost as soon as born. Woman, on the other hand, considers the means.'

They came, after three days' posting, to Manchester. They found it a beautiful city, situated on a clear sparkling stream, in the midst of delightful rural scenery, and regularly built after the modern manner in straight streets at right angles to each other: the air was peculiarly bright and bracing. 'I wanted very much,' said the Professor, 'to show you this place. You see how pretty and quiet a place it is; yet in the old times it had a population of half a million. It was perpetually black with smoke; there were hundreds of vast factories where the men worked from six in the morning until six at night. Their houses were huts—dirty, crowded nests of fever; their sole amusements were to smoke tobacco and to drink beer and spirits; they died at thirty worn out; they were of sickly and stunted appearance; they were habitual wife-beaters; they neglected their children; they had no education, no religion, no hopes, no wishes for anything but plentiful pipe and beer. See it now! The population reduced to twenty thousand; the factories swept away; the machinery destroyed; the men working separately each in his own house, making cotton for home consumption. Let us walk through the streets.'

These were broad, clean, and well kept. Very few persons were about. A few women lounged about the Court, or gathered together on the steps of the Town Hall, where one was giving her opinions violently on politics generally; some stood at the doorways talking to their neighbours; in the houses one could hear the steady click-click of the loom or spinning-jenny, as the man within, or the man and his sons, sat at their continuous and solitary labour.

'This is beautiful to think of, is it not?'

'I do not know what to say,' he replied. 'You ask me, after all that you have taught me, to admire a system in which men are slaves. Yet all looks well from the outside.'

'It began,' the Professor went on, without answering him directly, 'with the famous law of the "Clack" Parliament—that in which there were three times as many women as men—which enacted that wives should receive the wages of their husbands on Monday morning, and that unmarried men, unless they could be represented by mothers or sisters, or other female relations of whom they were the support, should be paid in kind, and be housed separately in barracks provided for the purpose, where discipline could be maintained. It was difficult at first to carry this legislation into effect: the men rebelled; but the law was enforced at last. That was the death-blow to the male supremacy. Woman, for the first time, got possession of the purse. What was done in Manchester was followed in other places. Young man, the spot you stand on is holy, or the reverse, whichever you please, because it is the birthplace of woman's sovereignty.

'Presently it began to be whispered abroad that the hours were too long, the work too hard, and the association of men together in such large numbers was dangerous. Then, little by little, wives withdrew their husbands from the works, mothers their sons, and set them up with spinning-jennies and looms at home. Hand-made cotton was protected; the machine-made was neglected. Soon the machines were silent and the factories closed; in course of time they were pulled down. Then other improvements followed. The population was enormously diminished, partly by the new laws which forbade the marriage of unhealthy or deformed men, and only allowed women to choose husbands when they had themselves obtained a certificate of good health and good conduct. Formerly the men married at nineteen; by the new laws they were compelled to wait until four-and-twenty; then, further, to wait until they were asked; and lastly, if they were asked, to obtain a certificate of soundness and freedom from any complaint which might be transmitted to children. Therefore as few of the Manchester workmen were quite free from some form of disease, the population rapidly decreased.'

'But,' said Lord Chester, 'is that wrong? A man ought to be healthy.'

That was, indeed, the creed in which he had been brought up.

'I am telling you the history of the place,' replied the Professor. 'Marriage being thus almost impossible, the Manchester women emigrated and the workmen stayed where they were, and gradually the weakly ones died out. As for the present Manchester man, you shall see him on Sunday when he goes to church.'

They stayed in this pleasant and countrified town for some days. On Sunday they went to the cathedral, and attended the service, which was conducted by the Bishop herself and her principal clergy. As the Bishop preached, Lord Chester looked about him, and watched the men. They were mostly a tall and handsome race, though, in the middle-aged men, the labour at the spindles had bowed their shoulders and contracted their chests. Their faces, however, like those of the London congregation, were listless and apathetic; they paid little heed to the sermon, yet devoutly knelt, bowed, and stood up at the right places. They seemed neither to feel nor to take any interest in life. Some of the women looked as if they interpreted the law of marital obedience in the strictest, even its harshest manner possible.

Lord Chester looked with a certain special curiosity at a regiment of young unmarried workmen. He had often enough before watched such a regiment passing to and from church, but never with such interest. For in these boys he had now learned to recognise the masters of the future.

They were mostly quite young, and naturally presented a more animated appearance than their married elders. Those of them who came from the country, or had no parents, were kept in a barrack under strict rule and discipline, having prescribed hours for gymnastics, exercises, and recreation, as well as for labour.

They were not all boys. Among them marched those whom unkind Nature or accident had set apart as condemned to celibacy. These were the consumptive, the asthmatic, the crippled, the humpbacked, the deformed; those who had inherited diseases of lung, brain, or blood; the unfortunates who could not marry, and who were, therefore, cared for with what was officially known as kindness. These poor creatures presented the appearance of the most hopeless misery. At other times Lord Chester would have passed them by without a thought. He knew now how different would have been their lot under a government which did not call itself maternal.

Neither boys nor incurables received pay, and the surplus of their work was devoted to the great Mother's Sustentation Fund, or, as it was called for short, the Mother's Tax. This was intended to supplement the wages earned by the husband at home in case of insufficiency. But the wives were exhorted and admonished to take care of their husbands, and keep them constantly at work.

'They do take care of them,' said the Professor. 'They make them clean up house, cook meals, and look after the children, as well as carry on their trade; while they themselves wrangle over politics in the street or in some of the squabble-halls, which are always open. The men never go out except on Sundays; they have no friends; they have no recreation.'

'But formerly they were even worse off, according to your own showing.'

'No; because if they were slaves to their wheels, they were slaves who worked in gangs, and they sometimes rose from the ranks. These men are solitary slaves who can never rise.'

'Is there nothing good at all?' cried the young man. 'Would you make a revolution, and upset everything? As for religion——'

'Say nothing,' said the Professor, 'about religion till I have shown you the old one. Yes; there was once something grander than anything you can imagine. We women, who have belittled everything, have even spoiled our religion.'

They passed a couple of young men wending their way to the gymnasium with racquets in their hands.

'They are the sons of the doctor or lawyer, I suppose,' said the Professor looking after them.

'Fine young fellows! But what are we to do with them? The law says that every boy, except the son of a peeress, shall learn a trade. No doubt these boys have learned a trade, but they do not practise it. They stay at home idle, or they spend their days in athletics. Some time or other they will marry a woman in their own rank, and then the rest of their lives will be devoted to managing the house and looking after the children, while their wives go to office and earn the family income.'

'What would you do with them?'

'Nay, Lord Chester; what will you do for them? That is the question.'

The next day they left Manchester, and proceeded on their journey. At Liverpool they saw seven miles of splendid old docks, lining the banks of the river; but there were no ships. The trade of the old days had long since left the place: it was a small town now with a few fishing smacks. The Professor enlarged upon the history of the past.

'But were the men happy?'

'I do not know. That is nowhere stated. I imagine there used to be happiness of a kind for men in forming part of a busy hive. At least the other plan—our plan—does not seem to produce much solid happiness....'

Gradually Lord Chester was being led to think less of the individual and more of his work. But it took time to eradicate his early impressions.

At Liverpool they visited the convict-prison—the largest prison in England. It was that prison specially devoted to the worst class of criminals—those undergoing life sentences for wife-beating. They found a place surrounded by a high wall and a deep ditch; they were admitted, on the Professor showing a pass, through a door at which a dozen female warders were sitting on duty. One of them was told off to conduct them round the prison. The convicts, coarsely clad in sackcloth, were engaged in perpetually doing unnecessary and profitless work—some dug holes which others filled up again; some carried heavy weights up ladders and down again,—there was the combined cruelty of monotony, of uselessness, and of excessive toil. In this prison—because physical force is necessary for men of violence—they had men as well as women for warders. These were stationed at intervals, and were armed with loaded guns and bayonets. It was well known that there was always great difficulty in persuading men to take this place, or to keep them when there. Mostly they were criminals of less degree, who purchased their liberty by becoming, for a term of years, convict-warders.

'No punishment too bad for wife-beaters,' said the Professor when they came away. 'What punishment is there for women who make slaves of their husbands, lock them up, kill them with work? or for old women who marry young men against their will?'

'You must clear out that den,' she went on, after a pause. 'A good many men are imprisoned there on the sole unsupported charge of their wives—innocent, no doubt; and if not innocent, then they have been punished enough.'

Lord Chester was being led gradually to regard himself, not as an intending rebel, but as a great reformer. Always the Professor spoke of the future as certain, and of his project, yet vague without a definite plan, as of a thing actually accomplished.

They left the dreary and deserted Liverpool, with its wretched convict-prison. They drove first across the country, which had once been covered with manufacturing towns, now all reduced to villages; they stopped at little country inns in places where there yet lingered traditions of former populousness; they passed sometimes gaunt ruins of vast brick buildings which had been factories; the roads were quiet and little used; the men they met were chiefly rustics going to or returning from their work; there was no activity, no traffic, no noise upon these silent highways.

'How can we ever restore the busy past?' asked Lord Chester.

'First release your men; let them work together; let them be taught; the old creative energy will waken again in the brains of men, and life will once more go forward. It will be for you to guide the movement when you have started it.'

As their journey drew to a conclusion, the Professor gave utterance, one by one, to several maxims of great value and importance:—

'Give men love,' she said; 'we women have killed love.'

'There is no love without imagination. Now the imagination cannot put forth its flowers but for the sake of young and beautiful women.'

'No true work without emulation; we have killed emulation.'

'No progress without ambition; we have killed ambition.'

'It is better to advance the knowledge of the world one inch than to win the long-jump with two-and-twenty feet.'

'Better vice than repression. A drunken man may be a lesson to keep his fellows sober.'

'Nothing great without suffering.'

'Strong arm, strong brain.'

'When women begin to invent they will justify their supremacy.'

'The Higher Intelligence is a phrase that must be transferred, not lost sight of.'

'Men who are happy laugh—they must laugh. Women, who have never felt the necessity of laughter, have killed it in men.'

'The sun is masculine—he creates. The moon is feminine—she only reflects.'

And so, with many other parables, dark sayings, and direct teachings, the wise woman brought her disciple to her own house at Cambridge.

CHAPTER VII.ON THE TRUMPINGTON ROAD

PROFESSOR INGLEBY lived on the Trumpington Road, about a mile and a quarter from the Senate House. Her residence was a large and handsome house shut in by a high wall, with extensive grounds, and surrounded by high trees, so that no one could see the garden from the main road. The house was a certain mystery to the girls who on Sundays took their constitutional to Trumpington and back. Some said that the Professor was ashamed of her husband, which was the reason why he was never seen, not even at Church; others said that she kept him in such rigid discipline that she refused the poor man permission even to walk outside the grounds of the house. Her two daughters, who regularly came to church with their mother, were pretty girls, but had a submissive gentle look quite strange among the turbulent young spirits of the University. They were never seen in society; and for some reason unknown to anybody except herself, the Professor refused to enter them at any college. Meantime no one was invited to the house: when one or two ladies tried to break through the reserve so strangely maintained by the most learned Professor in the University, and left their cards, the visit was formally returned by the Professor herself, accompanied by one of her girls. But things went no further, and invitations were neither accepted nor returned. It is therefore not surprising that this learned woman, who seemed guided by none of the motives which influence most women—who was not ambitious, who refused rank, who desired not money—gradually came to bear a mythical character. She was represented as an ogre: the undergraduates, always fond of making up stories, amused themselves by inventing legends about her home life and her autocratic rule. Some, however, said that the house was haunted, her husband off his head, and her daughters weak in their intellect. There was, therefore, some astonishment when it was announced officially that the Professor was bringing Lord Chester to stay at her own house—'in perfect seclusion,' added the paper, to the disgust of all Cambridge, who would have liked to make much of this interesting young peer. However, long vacation had begun when he came up, so that the few left were either the reading undergraduates or the dons.

'Here,' said the Professor, as she ushered her guest into a spacious hall, with doors opening into other rooms on either hand, 'you will find yourself in a house of the past. Nothing in my husband's house, or hardly anything, that is not two hundred years old at least; nothing which does not belong to the former dynasty: we use as little as possible that is new.'

Lord Chester looked about him: the hall was hung with pictures, and these were of a kind new to him, for they represented scenes in which man was not only the executive hand, but also the directing head, usurping to himself the functions of the Higher Intelligence. Thus Man was sitting on the Judicial Bench; Man was preaching in the Church; Man was holding debate in Parliament; Man was writing books; Man was studying. Where, then, was Woman? She was represented as spinning, sewing, nursing the baby, engaged in domestic pursuits, being wooed by young lovers, young herself, sitting among the children.

'You like our pictures?' asked the Professor. 'They were painted during the Subjection of Woman two hundred years ago. Men in those days worked for women; women gave men their love and sympathy: without love, which is a stimulus, labour is painful to man; without sympathy, which supports, labour is intolerable to him; with, or without, labour—necessary work with head or hand for the daily bread—is almost always intolerable to woman. Therefore, since the Great Revolution, there has been no good work done by man, and no work at all by women.'

She opened a door, holding the handle for a moment, as if with reverence for what was within. 'Here is our library,' she whispered. 'Come, let me present you to my husband. I warn you, beforehand, that our manners are like our furniture—old-fashioned.'

It was a large room, filled with books of ancient aspect: at a table sat, among his papers, a venerable old man, the like of whom Lord Chester had never seen before. It must be owned that the existing régime did not produce successful results in old men. They were too often frivolous or petulant; they were sometimes querulous; they complained of the want of respect with which they were treated, and yet generally neither said nor did anything worthy of respect.

But this was a dignified old man: thin white locks hung round his square forehead, beneath which were eyes still clear and full of kindliness; and his mobile lips parted with a peculiarly sweet smile when he greeted his guest. For the first time in his life, Lord Chester looked, with wonder, upon a man who bore in his face and his carriage the air of Authority.

The room was his study: the walls were hidden with books; the table was covered with papers. Strange, indeed, to see an old man in such a place, engaged in such pursuits!

'Be welcome,' he said, 'to my poor house. Your lordship has, I learn, been the pupil of my wife.'

'An apt and ready pupil,' she interposed, with meaning.

'I rejoice to hear it. You will now, if you please, be my pupil—for a short time only. You have much to learn, and but a brief space to learn it in before we proceed upon the Mission of which you know. Will you leave Lord Chester with me, my dear?'

The Professor left them alone.

'Sit down, my lord. I would first ask you a few questions.'

He questioned the young man with great care; ascertained that he knew already, having been taught in these late days by the Professor, the most important points of ancient history; that he was fully acquainted with his own pedigree, and what it meant; that he was filled with indignation and shame at the condition of his country; that he was ready to throw off the restraints and prejudices of Religion, and eager to become the Leader of the 'Great Revolt,' if he only knew how to begin.

'But,' said Lord Chester, stammering and confused, 'I shall want help—direction—even words. If the Professor——' he looked about in confusion.

'I will find you the help you want. Look to me, and to those who work with me, for guidance. This is a man's movement, and must be guided by men alone. Sufficient for the moment that we have in your lordship our true leader, that you will consent to be guided until you know enough to lead—and that you will be with us—to the very death, if that must be.'

'To the very death,' replied Lord Chester, holding out his hand.

'It is well that you should first know,' the old man went on, 'who I am, and to what hands you entrust your future. Learn, then, that by secret laying on of hands the ancient Episcopal Order hath been carried on, and continues unto this day. Though there are now but two or three Bishops remaining of the old Church, I am one—the Bishop of London. This library contains the theology of our Church—the works of the Fathers. The Old Faith shall be taught to you—the faith of your wise fathers.'

Lord Chester stared; for the Professor had told him nothing of this.

'You may judge of all things,' said the Bishop, 'by their fruits. You have seen the fruits of the New Religion: you have gone through the length and the breadth of the land, and have found whither the superstition of the Perfect Woman leads. I shall teach you the nobler Creed, the higher Faith,—that'—here his voice lowered, and his eyes were raised—'that, my son, of the Perfect Man—the Divine Man.

'And now,' he went on, after a pause, ringing the bell, 'I want to introduce to you some of your future officers and followers.'

There appeared in answer to this summons a small band of half a dozen young men. Among them, to Lord Chester's amazement, were two friends of his own, the very last men whom he would have expected to meet. They were Algy Dunquerque, the young fellow we have already mentioned, and a certain Jack Kennion, as good a rider, cricketer, and racquet-player as any in the country. These two men in the plot? Had he been walking and living among conspirators? The two entered, but they said nothing. Yet the look of satisfaction on their faces spoke volumes.

'Gentlemen,' said the Bishop, 'I desire to present you to the Earl of Chester. In this house and among ourselves he is already what he will shortly be to the whole world—His Royal Highness the Earl of Chester, heir to the crown—nay—actual King of England. The day long dreamed of among us, my children—the day for which we have worked and planned—has arrived. Before us stands the Chief, willing and ready to lead the Cause in person.'

They bowed profoundly. Then each one advanced in turn, took his hand, and murmured words of allegiance.

The first was a tall thin young man of four-and-twenty, with eager eyes, pale face, and high narrow forehead, named Clarence Veysey. 'If you are what we hope and pray,' he said, looking him full in the face with searching gaze, 'we are your servants to the death. If you are not, God help England and the Holy Faith!'

The next who stepped forward was Jack Kennion. He was a young man of his own age, of great muscular development, with square head, curly locks, and laughing eyes. He held out his hand and laughed. 'As for me,' he said, 'I have no doubt as to what you are. We have waited for you a long time, but we have you at last.'

The next was Algy Dunquerque.

'I told you,' he said laughing, 'that I was ready to follow you. But I did not hope or expect to be called upon so soon. Something, of course, I knew, because I am a pupil of the Bishop, and knew how long Professor Ingleby has been working upon your mind. At last, then!' He heaved a mighty sigh of satisfaction, and then began to laugh. 'Ho, ho! Think of the flutter among the petticoats! Think of the debates in the House! Think of the excommunications!'

One after the other shook hands, and then the Bishop spoke, as if interpreting the thought of all. 'This day,' he said, 'is the beginning of new things. We shall recall the grandeurs of the past, which no living man can remember. Time was when we were a mighty country, the first in the world: we had the true Religion, two thousand years old; a grand state Church; we had an ancient dynasty and a constitutional monarchy; we had a stately aristocracy always open to new families; we had an immense commerce; we had flourishing factories; we had great and loyal colonies; we had a dense and contented population; we had enormous wealth; science in every branch was advancing; there was personal freedom; every man could raise himself from the lowest to the highest rank; there was no post too high for the ambition of a clever lad. In those days Man was in command.

'Let us,' he continued, after a pause, 'think how all this has been changed. We have lost our reigning family, and have neither king nor queen; we have thrown away our old hereditary aristocracy, and replaced it by a false and pretentious House, in which the old titles have descended through a line of women, and the new ones have been created for the noisiest of the first female legislators; we have abolished our House of Commons, and given all the power to the Peeresses; we have lost the old worship, and invented a creed which has not even the merit of commanding the respect of those who are most interested in keeping it up. Does any educated woman now believe in the Perfect Woman, except as a means of keeping men down?

'As for our trade, it is gone; as for our greatness, it is gone; as for our industries, they are gone; as for our arts, they have perished: we stand alone, the contempt of the world to whom we are no longer a Power. Our men are kept in ignorance; they are forbidden to rise, by their own work, from one class to another; class and caste distinctions are deepened, and differences in rank are multiplied; there is no more science; electricity, steam, heat, and air are the servants of man no longer; men cannot learn; they are even forbidden to meet together; they have lost the art of self-government; they are cowed; they are cursed with a false religion; they have no longer any hopes or any aims.

'Fortunately,' he continued, 'they have left man something: he has retained his strength; they have even legislated with the view of keeping him healthy and strong. In your strength, my sons, shall you prosper. But you will have to revive the old spirit. That will be the most difficult—the only difficult—task. Take Lord Chester away now, my children, and show him our relics of the past.'

In the room next to the library was a collection of strange and wonderful things, all new and unintelligible to Lord Chester. Jack Kennion acted as exhibitor.

'These,' he said, 'are chiefly models of the old machinery. I study them daily, in the hope of restoring the mechanical skill of the past. These engines with multitudinous wheels which are so intricate to look at, and yet so simple in their action, formerly served to keep great factories at work, and found occupation for hundreds and thousands of men; these black round boxes were steam machines which dragged long trains full of people about the country at the rate of sixty miles an hour; these glittering things in brass were made to illustrate knowledge which has long since died out, unless I can recover it by the aid of the old books; these complicated things were weapons among us when science ruled everything; all these books treat of the forgotten knowledge; these paintings on the wall show the life of the very world as it was when men ruled it; these maps showed the former greatness of the country: everything here proves from what a height we have fallen. And to think that it is only here—in this one house of all England—that we can feel what we once were,—what we will be—yes, we will be—again.'

His eyes were lit with fire, his cheeks aflame as he spoke.

During the talk of this afternoon, Lord Chester discovered that the education of every one of these young men had been conducted with a view to his future work in or after the Revolution. Thus Algernon Dunquerque was learned in the old arts of drilling and ordering masses of men. Jack Kennion had studied mechanics and mathematics; another had learned ancient law and history; another had been trained to speak,—and so on. Clarence Veysey, for his part, had been taught by the Bishop the Mysteries of the Old Religion, and was an ordained Priest. These things the new recruit made out from the eager talk of his friends, who seemed all of them anxious to instruct him at once in everything they knew.

It was a relief at last, when the first bell rang, to be alone for a few minutes, if only to get his ideas cleared a little. What had he learned since he left London? What was before him? Anyhow, change, action, freedom.

He found the Professor and her daughters in the drawing-room. The girls received him with smiles of welcome. The elder, Grace—a girl whose sweetness of face was new to Lord Chester, accustomed to the hard lines which a life of combat so early brings upon a woman's eyes and brow—had, which was the first thing he noticed in her, large, clear gray eyes of singular purity. The other, Faith, was smaller, slighter, and perhaps more lovely, though in a different way, a less spiritual fashion. Both, in the outer world would have been considered painfully shy. Lord Chester was beginning to consider shyness as a virtue in women. At all events, it was a quality rarely experienced outside.

He was already prepared for many changes, and for customs new to him. Yet he was hardly ready for the complete reversal of social rules as he experienced at this dinner. For the subjects of talk were started by the men, who almost monopolised the conversation; while the ladies merely threw in a word here and there, which served as a stimulus, and showed appreciation rather than a desire to join in the argument. And such talk! He had been accustomed to hear the ladies talk almost uninterruptedly of politics—that is, of personal matters, squabbles in the House, disputes about precedence, intrigues for title and higher rank—and dress. Nothing else, as a rule, occupied the dinner-table. The men, who rarely spoke, were occasionally questioned about some cricket-match, some long race, or some other kind of athletics. This was due to politeness only, however; for, the question put and answered, the questioner showed how little interest she took in the subject by instantly returning to the subject previously in discussion. But at this table,—the Professor's—no, the Bishop's table,—the men talked of art, and in terms which Lord Chester could not understand. Nevertheless, he gathered that the so-called art of the Academicians was a thing absolutely beneath contempt. They talked of science, especially the square-headed youth Jack Kennion, to whom they deferred as to an authority; and he spoke of subjects, forms, and laws of which Lord Chester was absolutely ignorant: they talked of history, and all, including the Bishop's daughters—strange, how easily the new proselyte fell into the way of considering how the highest education is best fitted for men!—showed as intimate an acquaintance with the past as the Professor herself. They talked of religion; and here all deferred to the Bishop, who, while he spoke with authority, invited discussion. Strangest thing of all!—every man spoke as if his own opinion were worth considering. There was not the slightest deference to authority. The great and standard work of Cornelia Nipper on Political Economy, in which she summed up all that has been said, and left, as was taught at Cambridge, nothing more to be said; the Encyclopædia of Science, written by Isabella Bunter, in which she showed the absurdity of pushing knowledge into worthless regions; the sermons and dogmas of the illustrious and Reverend Violet Swandown, considered by the orthodox as containing guidance and comfort for the soul under all possible circumstances,—these works were openly scoffed at and derided.

Lord Chester said little; the conversation was for the most part beyond him. At his side sat the Bishop's elder daughter, Grace—a young lady of twenty-one or twenty-two, of a type strange to him. She had a singularly quiet, graceful manner; she listened with intelligent pleasure, and showed her appreciation by smiles rather than by words; when she spoke, it was in low tones, yet without hesitation; she was almost extravagantly deferent to her father, but towards her mother showed the affection of a loved and trusted companion. It was too much the custom in society for girls to show no regard whatever for the opinions or the wishes of their fathers.

The younger daughter, Faith, talked less; but Lord Chester noticed that as she sat next to Algy Dunquerque, that young man frequently ceased to join in the general conversation, and exchanged whispers with her; and they were whispers which made her eyes to soften and her cheek to glow. Good; in the new state of things the men would do the wooing for themselves. He thought of Constance, and wished she had been there.

When the ladies retired, the Bishop began to talk of the Great Cause.

'Your training,' he said to Lord Chester, 'has been, by my directions, that of a Prince rather than a private gentleman. That is to say, you have been taught a great many things, but you have not become a specialist. These friends of ours,'—he pointed to his group of disciples,—'are, each in his own line, better than yourself, and better than you will ever try to become. A Prince should be a patron of art, learning, and science and literature; but it does not become him to be an artist, a scholar, a philosopher, or a poet. You must be contented to sit outside the circle, so to speak. Now let us speak of our chances.'

He proceeded to discuss the best way of raising the country. His plan was a simultaneous revolt in half a dozen country districts; an appeal to the rustics; the union of forces; the seizure of towns; continual preaching and exhortation for the men; repression for the women; the destruction of their sacred pictures and figures; but no violence—above all, no violence. The Bishop was an ecclesiastic, and he was a recluse. He therefore did not understand what men are like when the passion of fighting is roused in them. He dreamed of a bloodless Revolution; he pictured the men voluntarily confessing the wisdom and the truth of the Old Religion. The event proved that all human institutions rest on force, and cannot be upset without the employment of force. To be sure, women cannot fight; but they had on their side the aid of superstition and the strong arms of the men whom they led in superstitious chains.

Upstairs one of the girls played and sang old songs: the words were strange; words and air went direct to the heart. Lord Chester listened disturbed and anxious, yet exultant.

The Professor pressed his hand.

'It is death or success,' she whispered. 'Be of good cheer; in either event you shall be counted noble among the men to come.'

When Grace Ingleby wished him good-night, she held his hand in hers with the firm grasp of a sister.

'You are one of us,' she said frankly. 'In this house we are all brothers and sisters in hope and in Religion. And if they found us out,' she added with a laugh, 'we should be brothers and sisters in death. Courage, my lord! There is all to gain.'

Faith Ingleby, the younger sister, who had less ardour for the Cause than for the men who were pledged to it, whispered low, as he took her hand,—

'We know all about Lady Carlyon; and we pray daily for her, and for you. Mother says she is worthy to become—to be raised—to be——'

'What?' he asked, reddening; for the girl hesitated and looked at him with a kind of awe.

'Queen of England.'

'Don't anticipate, Faith,' said Algy. 'Considering, however, what we have come out of, it strikes me that we have nothing to lose, whatever we may gain. Come, Chester, we want to have a quiet talk together as soon as the Bishop goes to bed.'

They talked for nearly the whole night. There was so much to say; one subject after another was started; there were so many chances to consider,—that it was four o'clock when they parted. Algy found, somewhere or other, a bottle of champagne.

'Come,' he cried, 'a stirrup-cup! I drink to the day when the "King shall enjoy his own again."'

'Algy!' said Lord Chester. 'To think that you have deceived me!'

'To think,' he replied laughing, 'that we have dreamed of this day so long! What would our Revolution be worth unless we were to have our hereditary and rightful king for leader! Yet, I confess it was hard to see you drawn daily closer to us, and not to hold out hands to drag you in—long ago. Yes, the Professor was right. She is always right. She glories in her obedience to the Bishop, but—whisper,—we all know very well that the Bishop does nothing without consulting her first, and nothing that she does not agree with. Don't be too sure, dear boy, about the Supremacy of Man.'

CHAPTER VIII. THE BISHOP

AT seven in the morning, Lord Chester was roused from an extremely disagreeable dream. He was, in this vision, being led off to execution, in company with the Bishop, Constance, the Professor, and Grace Ingleby. The Duchess of Dunstanburgh headed the procession, carrying the ropes in her own illustrious hand. Her face was terrible in its sternness. The Chancellor was there, pointing skinny fingers, and saying 'Yah!' Before him, within five minutes' walk, stood five tall and comely gallows, with running tackle beautifully arranged; also, in case there should be any preference expressed by the criminals for fancy methods of execution, there were stakes and fagots, guillotines, wheels to be broken upon, men with masks, and other accessories of public execution.

It was therefore a relief, on opening his eyes, to discover that he was as yet only a peaceful guest of Professor Ingleby, and that the Great Revolt had not yet begun. 'At all events,' he said cheerfully, 'I shall have the excitement of the attempt, if I am to be hanged or beheaded for it. And most certainly it will be less disagreeable to be hanged than to marry the Duchess. Perhaps even there may be, if one is lucky, an opportunity of telling her so. A last dying speech of that kind would be popular.'

Shaking off gloomy thoughts, therefore, he dressed hastily, and descended to the Hall, where most of the party of the preceding night were collected, waiting for him. The tinkling of a bell which had awakened him now began again. Algy Dunquerque told him it was the bell for chapel. 'But,' he added, 'don't be afraid. It is not the kind of service we are accustomed to. There is no homily on obedience; and, thank goodness, there is no Perfect Woman here!'

The chapel was a long room, fitted simply with a few benches, a table at the east end, a brass eagle for lectern, and some books. The Professor and the girls were already in their places, and in a few moments the Bishop himself appeared, in lawn-sleeves and surplice.

For the first time Lord Chester witnessed the spectacle of a man conducting the services. It gave a little shock and a momentary sense of shame, which he shook off as unworthy. A greater shock was the simple service of the Ancient Faith which followed.

To begin with, there were no flowers, no incense girls, no anthems, no pictures of Sainted

Women, no figures of the Holy Mother, no veiled Perfect Woman on an altar crowned with roses; and there were no genuflections, no symbolical robes, no mystic whisperings, no change of dress, no pretence at mysterious powers. All was perfectly simple—a few prayers, a lesson from a great book, a hymn, and then a short address.

The Ancient Faith had long since become a thing dim and misty, and wellnigh forgotten save to a few students. Most knew of it only as an obsolete form of religion which belonged to the semi-barbarism of Man's supremacy: it had been superseded by the fuller revelation of the Perfect Woman,—imposed, so to speak, upon the world for the elevation of women into their proper place, and for the guidance of subject man. It was carefully taught with catechism, articles, doctrines, and history, to children as soon as they could run about. It was now a settled Faith, venerable by reason of its endowments and dignities rather than its age, supported by all the women of England, defended on historical and intellectual grounds by thousands of pens, by weekly sermons, by domestic prayers, by maternal admonitions, by the terrors of the after-world, by the hopes of that which is present with us. A great theological literature had grown up around the Faith. It was the only recognised and tolerated religion; it was not only the religion of the State, but also the very basis of the political constitution. For as the Perfect Woman was the goddess whom they worshipped, the Peeresses who ruled were rulers by divine right, and the Commons—before that House had been abolished—were members of their House by divine permission: every member officially described herself a member by divine permission. To dispute about the authority of the ecclesiastical Decrees which came direct from the Upper House, was blasphemy, a criminal offence, and punishable by death; and to deny the authority of the Decrees was to incur certain death. It is not, therefore, surprising to hear that there was neither infidelity nor nonconformity in the whole country. On the other hand, because there must be some outlet for private and independent opinion, there were many interpretations of the law, and opinions as many and as various as those who disputed concerning the right interpretation. Under the rule of woman, there could be no doubt, no compromise, no dispute, on essentials. The principles of religion, like those of moral, social, and political economy, were fixed and unalterable; they were of absolute certainty. As to the Articles of Religion, as to the Great Dogma of the Revealed Perfect Woman, there could be no doubt, no discussion.

And now, after a most religious training, Lord Chester—a man who ought to have accepted and obeyed in meekness—was actually assisting, in a spirit half curious, half converted, at a service in which the Perfect Woman was entirely left out. What next? and next?

Ever since Lord Chester had become awakened to the degradation of man and the possibility of his restoration, his mind had been continually exercised by the absolute impossibility of reconciling his new Cause with his Religion. How could the Grand Revolt be carried out in the teeth of the most sacred commandments? How could he remain a faithful servant of the Church, and yet rebel against the first law of the Church? How could he continue to worship the Perfect Woman when he was thrusting woman out of her place? We may suppose Cromwell, by way of parallel, trying to reconcile the divine right of kings with the execution of Charles the First.

Here, however, though as yet he understood it not, there was a service which absolutely ignored the Perfect Woman. The prayers were addressed direct to the Eternal Father as the Father. The language was plain and simple. The words of the hymn which they sang were strong and simple, ringing true as if from the heart, like the hammer on the anvil.

The Bishop closed his book, bowed his head for a few moments in silent prayer, then rose and addressed his congregation; and, as he spoke, the young men clasped hands, and the girls sobbed.

'Beloved,' he began, 'at this moment it would be strange indeed if our hearts were not moved within us—if our prayers and praises were not spontaneous. Let us remember that we are the descendants of those who handed down the lamp in secrecy from one to the other, always with prayer that they might live to see the Day of Restoration. The Day of Attempt, indeed, is, nigh at hand. We pray with all our hearts that we may bring the Return of the Light of the World. Then may those who witness the glorious sight cry aloud to depart in peace, because there will be nothing more for them to pray for. What better thing could there be for us, my children, than to die in this attempt?

'You who have learned the story of the past; you who worship with me in the great and simple Faith of your ancestors; you who know how man did wondrous deeds in the days of old, and how he fell and became a slave, who was created to be master; you who are ready to begin the upward struggle; you who are the apostles of the Old Order,—children of the Promise, go forth in your strength and conquer.'

Then he gave them the Benediction, and the service was concluded.

Half an hour afterwards, when the emotions of this act of worship were somewhat calmed, they met at breakfast. The girls' eyes were red, and the young men were grave; but the conversation flowed in the accustomed grooves.

After breakfast, Lord Chester was intrusted to the care of the pale and austere young man who had been first presented to him.

'Clarence Veysey,' said the Bishop, 'is my secretary, my private chaplain, and my pupil. He is himself in full priest's orders, and will instruct you in the rudiments of our Faith. We do not substitute one authority for another, Lord Chester. You will be exhorted to try and examine for yourself the doctrines before you accept them. Yet you will understand that what you are taught stood the test of question, doubt, and attack for more than two thousand years before it was violently torn from mankind. Go, my son, receive instruction with docility; but do not fear to question and to doubt.'

'I am indeed a priest,' said Clarence Veysey, taking him into the library. 'I have been judged worthy of the laying on of hands.'

'And do not your friends know or suspect?'

'No,' he replied. 'It is, in fact'—here he blushed and hesitated—'a position of great difficulty. I must, perforce, until we are ripe for action, act a deceptive part. The necessity for concealment is a terrible thing. Yet, what help? One remembers him who bowed himself in the House of Rimmon.'

'The concealment,' said Lord Chester, unfeelingly, because he knew nothing about Naaman, 'would be part of the fun.'

'The fun?' this young priest gasped. 'But, of course—you do not know. We are in deadly earnest, and he calls it—fun: we strive for the return of the world to the Faith, and he calls it—fun!'

'I beg your pardon,' said Lord Chester. 'I seem—I hardly know why—to have offended you. I really think it must be very good fun to have this pretty secret all to yourself when you are at home.'

'Oh! he is very—very ignorant,' cried Clarence.

'Well——' Lord Chester did not mind being instructed by the old Bishop or by the Professor. But the superiority of this smooth-cheeked youth of his own age galled him. Nevertheless, he saw that the young priest was deeply in earnest, and he restrained himself.

'Teach me, then,' he said.

'As for the deception,' said Clarence, 'it is horrible. One falsehood leads to another. I pretend weakness—even disease and pain—to escape being married to some one; because what can a man of my position—of the middle class—do to earn my bread? Then I have simulated sinful paroxysms of bad temper. This keeps women away: so long as I am believed to be ill-tempered and sickly, of course no one will offer to marry me. A reputation of ill-temper is, fortunately, the best safeguard possible for a young man who would possess his soul in freedom. I try to persuade myself that necessary deception is harmless deception; and if we succeed——' he paused and sighed. 'Come, my lord, let me teach you something of the true Faith.'

They spent the whole morning together, while Clarence Veysey unfolded the mysteries of the Ancient Faith, and showed how divine a thing it was, and how fitted for every possible phase or emergency of life. His earnestness, the sincerity and honesty of his belief, deeply moved Lord Chester.

'But how,' asked the neophyte, 'came this wonderful religion to be lost?'

'It was thrown away, not lost,' replied the priest. 'Even before the women began to encroach upon the power of men, it was thrown away. Had the Ancient Faith survived, we should have been spared the coming struggle. It was thrown away. Men themselves threw it away—some wilfully, others through weakness—receiving forms and the pretensions of priests instead of the substance; so that they surrendered their liberty, put the priest between themselves and the Father, practised the servile rite of confession, and went on to substitute the image of the Mother and Child upon their altars, in place of the Divine Manhood, whose image had been in their fathers' hearts. Why, when after many years it was resolved to place on every altar the Veiled Figure of the Perfect Woman, the very thought of the Divine Man had been wellnigh forgotten. 'But not lost,' he went on in a kind of rapture—'not lost. He lingers still among us—here in this most sacred house. He is spoken of in rustic speech; He lingers in rustic traditions; many a custom still survives, the origin of which is now forgotten, which speaks to us who knew of the dear old Faith.'

He spoke more of this old Faith,—the only solution, he declared, ever offered, of the problem of life,—the ever-living Divine Brother, always compassionate, always helping, always lifting higher the souls of those who believe.

'See!' cried the enthusiast, falling on his knees, 'He is here. O Christ—Lord—Redeemer, Thou art with us—yea, always and always!'

When he brought Lord Chester again into the presence of the Bishop, they both had tears in their eyes.

'He comes, my lord,' said Clarence, a sober exultation in his voice—'he comes as a catechumen, seeking instruction and baptism.'

Needless here to relate by what arguments, what teaching, Lord Chester became a convert to the New Faith; nor how he was baptized, nor with what ardour he entered into the doctrines of a religion the entrance to which seemed like the bursting of prison-doors, the breaking of fetters, the sudden rush of light. His new friends became, in a deeper sense, his brothers and his sisters. They were of the same religion; they worshipped God through the revelation of the Divine Man.

Then followed a quiet time of study, talk, and preparation, during which Lord Chester remained in perfect seclusion, and went into no kind of society. Professor Ingleby reported to Lady Boltons that her ward went nowhere, desired no other companionship, amused himself with reading, made no reference whatever to the Duchess or Lady Carlyon, and appeared to be perfectly happy, in his 'quietest and most delightful manner.' The letter was forwarded by Lady Boltons to the Chancellor, and by her to the Duchess, who graciously expressed her approbation of the young man's conduct. There was thus not the least suspicion. On Sunday, which was a day of great danger, because the young men were growing impatient of restraint, Lord Chester went to church with the Professor and her daughters.

Here, while the organ pealed among the venerable aisles of the University Church, while the clouds of incense rolled about before the Veiled Statue on the altar, while the hymn was lifted, while the preacher in shrill tones defended a knotty point in theology, while the dons and heads of houses slumbered in their places, while the few undergraduates remaining up for the Long leaned over the gallery and looked about among the men below for some handsome face to admire, Lord Chester sat motionless, gazing straight before him, obedient to the form, with his thoughts far away.

The strangeness of the new life passed away quickly; the outside life, the repression and pretence, were forgotten, or only remembered with indignation. These young men were free; they laughed—a thing almost unknown under a system when a jest was considered as necessarily either rude or scoffing, certainly ill-bred—they laughed continually; they made up stories; they related things which they had read. Algy Dunquerque, who was an actor, made a little comedy of the Chancellor and the Duchess; and another of the trial and execution of the rebels, showing the fortitude of Clarence Veysey and the unwillingness of himself; and another on the arguments for the Perfect Government. They sat up late; they drank wine and sang songs; they talked of love and courtship; above all, they read the old books.

Think of their joy, when they found on the shelves Shakespeare, Rabelais, Fielding, Smollett, and Dickens! Think of their laughter when they read aloud those rude and boisterous writers, who respected nothing, not even marriage, and had never heard of any Perfect Woman at all! Think, too, of their delight when the words of wisdom went home to them; when they reflected on the great and wise Pantagruel, followed the voyagers among the islands of Humanity, or watched over the career of Hamlet, the maddened Prince of Denmark! These were for their leisure hours, but serious business occupied the greater part of the day.

Continually, also, the young men held counsel together, and discussed their plans. It was known that the rising would take place at the earliest possible opportunity. But two difficulties presented themselves. What would constitute a favourable opportunity? and what would be the best way to take advantage of it?

Algy Dunquerque insisted, for his part, that they should ride through the country, calling on the men to rise and follow. What, however, if the men refused to rise and follow?

Jack Kennion thought they should organise a small body first, drill and arm them, and then seize upon a place and hold it. Clarence Veysey thought that he was himself able, book in hand, to persuade the whole of the country.

For men to rise against women seems, since the event, a ridiculously easy thing. As a matter of fact, it was an extremely difficult thing. For the men had been so kept apart that they did not know how to act together, and so kept in subjection that they were cowed. The prestige of the ruling sex was a factor of the very highest importance. It was established, not only by law, but by religion. How ask men to rebel when their eternal interests demanded submission? Men, again, had no longer any hope of change. While the present seems unalterable, no reform can ever be attempted. Life was dull and monotonous; but how could it be otherwise? Men had ceased to ask if a change was possible. And the fighting spirit had left them; they were strong, of course, but their strength was that of the patient ox.

If there was to be fighting, the material on the side of the Government consisted first of the Horse Guards—three regiments, beautifully mounted and accoutred in splendid uniforms—every man a tall handsome fellow six feet high. These soldiers formed the escort at all great Functions. They never left London; they enjoyed a very fair social consideration; some of them were married to ladies of good family, and all were married well; they were commanded from the War Office by a department of a hundred secretaries, clerks, and copying-women.

Would they fight for the Government? or would they come over? At present no one could tell.

In addition to these regiments, the nation, which had no real standing army, maintained a force of constabulary for prison-warders. It has been already stated that the prisons were crowded with desperadoes and violent persons convicted of wife-beating, boxing their wives' ears, pulling their hair, and otherwise ill-treating them against the religion and law. They were coerced and kept in order by some fifteen or twenty thousand of the constabulary, who were drilled and trained, commanded by men chosen from their own ranks as sergeants, and armed with loaded rifles. It is true that the men were recruited from the lowest class—many of them being thieves, common rogues, and jailbirds, some of them having even volunteered as an exchange from prison; their pay was low, their fare poor; no woman of respectability would marry one of them; they were rude, fierce, and ill-disciplined; they frequently ill-treated the prisoners; and their superior officers—women who commanded from the rooms of a department—had no control whatever over them. They would probably fight, if only for the contempt and hatred in which they were held by men.

Where, for their own part, could they look for soldiers?

There were the rustics. They were strong, healthy, accustomed to work together, outspoken, never more than half-convinced of the superiority of women, practising the duty of obedience no more than they were obliged, fain to go courting on their own account, the despair of preachers, who were constantly taunted with the ill success of their efforts. Why, it was common—in some cases it was the rule—to find the woman in the cottage that most contemptible thing—a man-pecked wife. What was the good of paying wages to this wife, when her husband took from her what he wanted for himself? What was the good of making laws that men should not be abroad alone after dark, when in most of the English villages the men stood loitering and talking together in the streets till bed-time? What was the use of prohibiting all intoxicating drinks, when in every village there were some women who made beer and sold it to all the men who could pay for it, and though perfectly well known, were never denounced?

'They are ready to our hand,' said Lord Chester. 'The only question is, how to raise them, and how to arm them when they are raised.'

CHAPTER IX. THE GREAT CONSPIRACY

ONE morning, after six weeks of this pleasant life, Lord Chester, who had made excellent use of his time, and was now as completely a man as his companions, was summoned to the Bishop's study, and there received a communication of the greatest importance.

The Professor was the only other person present.

'I have thought it prudent, Lord Chester,' said the Bishop gravely, 'to acquaint you with the fact that the time is now approaching when the great Attempt will be made. Are you still of the same mind? May we look for your devotion—even if we fail?'

'You may, my lord.' The young man held out his hand, which the aged Bishop clasped.

'It is good,' he said, 'to see the devotion of youth ready to renounce life and its joys; to incur the perils of death and dishonour. This seems hard even in old age, when life has given all it has to give. But in young men—— Yet, my son, remember that the martyr does but change a lower life for a higher.'

'I give you my life, if so it must be,' Lord Chester repeated.

'We take what is offered cheerfully. You must know then, my lord, that the ground has been artfully prepared for us. This conspiracy, which you have hitherto thought confined to one old man's house and half a dozen young men living with him, is in reality spread over the whole country. We have organisations, great or small, in nearly every town of England. Some of them have as yet only advanced to the stage of discontent; others have been pushed on to learn that the evil condition of men is due chiefly to the government of women; others have learned that the sex which rules ought to obey; others, that the worship of the Perfect Woman is a vain superstition: none have gone so far as you and your friends, who have learned more—the faith in the Perfect Man. That is because you are to be the leaders, you yourself to be the Chief.

'Now, my lord, the thing having so far advanced, the danger is, that one or other of our secret societies may be discovered. True, they do not know the ramifications or extent of the conspiracy. They cannot, therefore, do us any injury by treachery or unlucky disclosures; yet the punishment of the members would be so severe as to strike terror into the rest of our members. Therefore, it is desirable to begin as soon as possible.'

'To-day!' cried the young Chief.

'No—not to-day, nor to-morrow. The difficulty is, to find some pretext,—some reasonable pretext—under cover of which we might rise.'

'Can we not invent something.'

'There are the convicts. We might raise a force, and liberate those of the prisoners who are victims of the harsh laws of violence and the refusal to take a husband's evidence when accused by a wife. Then the country would be with us. But I shrink from commencing this great rebellion with bloodshed.'

He paused and reflected for a time.

'Then there is the labour cry. We might send our little force into the towns, and call on the workmen to rise for freedom. But suppose they would not rise? Then—more bloodshed.

'Or we might preach the Faith throughout the land, as Clarence Veysey wants to do. But I incline not to the belief in wholesale miracles, and the age of faith is past, and the number of our preachers is very small.'

'You will be helped,' said the Professor, 'in a quarter where you least suspect. I, too, with my girls, have done my little.'

She proceeded to open a packet of papers, which she laid before the young Chief.

'What are these?' he asked.

'They are called Tracts for the Times,' she replied. 'They are addressed to the Women of England.'

He took them up and read them carefully one by one.

'Who wrote these?'

'The girls and I together. We posted them wherever we could get addresses—to all the undergraduates, to all the students of hospitals, Inns of Court, and institutions of every kind; to quiet country vicarages; to rich people and poor people,—wherever there was a chance, we directed a tract.'

'You have done well,' said the Bishop.

'They have been found out, and a reward is offered for the printers. As they were printed in the cellars of this house, the reward is not likely to be claimed. They were all posted here, which makes the Government the more uneasy. They believe in the spread of what they call irreligion among the undergraduates. Unfortunately, the undergraduates are as yet only discontented, because all avenues are choked.'

The Bishop took up one of the tracts again, and read it thoughtfully. It was headed, Tracts for the Times: For Young Women, and was the first number. The second title was Work and Women. The writer, in brief telling paragraphs, very different from the long-winded, verbose style everywhere prevalent, called upon women seriously to consider their own position, and the state that things had been brought to by the Government of the Peeresses. Every profession was crowded: the shameful spectacle of women begging for employment, even the most ill-paid, was everywhere seen; the law in both branches was filled with briefless and clientless members; there were more doctors than patients; there were more teachers than pupils; there were artists without number who produced acres of painted canvas every year and found no patrons; the Church had too many curates; while architects, journalists, novelists, poets, orators, swarmed, and were all alike ravenous for work at any rate of pay, even the lowest. The happiest were the few who could win their way by competitive examination into the Civil Service; and even there, the Government having logically applied the sound political axioms of supply and demand to the hire of their servants, they could hardly live upon their miserable pay, and must give up all hopes of marriage. There was a time, the tract went on, when men had to do all the work, including the work of the professions. In those days all kinds of work were considered respectable, so that there was not this universal run upon the professions. And in those days, said the writer, the axiom of open competition in professional charges was not acted up to, insomuch that physicians, barristers, and solicitors charged a sum agreed upon by themselves—and that an adequate sum—for services rendered; while the pay of the Service was given in consideration to the amount required for comfortable living. The only way out of the difficulty, concluded the author, was to limit the number of those who entered the professions, to regulate the charges on a liberal scale, and to increase the pay of the Services. As for the rest, if women must work, they must do the things which women can do well—sew, make dresses, cook, and, in fact, perform all those services which were thought menial, unless, indeed, they preferred the hard work of men in the fields and at the looms.

The second tract treated of the Idleness of Men.

By the wisdom of their ancestors, it had been ordained that every man should be taught a handicraft, by means of which to earn his own living. This wholesome rule had been allowed to fall into abeyance; for while some sort of carpenter's work was nominally and officially taught in boys' schools, it had long been considered a mark of social inferiority for man to do any work at all. 'We educate our men,' the tract went on, 'in the practice of every gymnastic and athletic feat; we turn them out strong, active, able to do and endure, and then we find nothing for them to do. Is it their fault that they become vacuous, ill-tempered, discontented, the bane of the house which their virtues ought to make a happy home? What else can we expect? Whence the early falling off into fat cheeks and flabby limbs? whence the love of the table—that vice which stains our manhood? whence the apathy at Church services?—whence should they come but from the forced idleness, the lack of interest in life?'

The tract went on to call for a reform in this as in other matters. Let the men be set to work; let men of all classes have to work. Why should women do all, as well as think for all? 'It must be considered, again, that every man cannot be married; indeed, under the present state of things few women can think of marriage till they have arrived at middle age, and therefore most men must remain single. Why should we doom them to a long life of forced inaction? Happier far the rustic who ploughs the field, or the cobbler who patches the village boots.' Then there followed an artful and specious reference to old times: 'Under the former régime, men worked, and women, in the freedom of the house, thought. The nominal ruler was the Hand; the actual, the Head. In those days, the flower of woman's life was not wasted in study and competition. The maidens were wooed while they were young and beautiful; their lovers worked for them, surrounded them with pleasant things, lapped them in warmth, brought them all that they could desire, made their lives a restful dream of love. It has come to this, O women of the New Faith, that you have thrown away the love of men, and with it the whole joy of creation! You worship the Woman; your mothers, happier in their generation, were contented each to be worshipped by a man.'

'That is very good,' said the Bishop.

Then the Professor produced another and a more dangerous manifesto, addressed to the young men of England. It was dark and mysterious: it bade them be on the watch for a great and glorious change; they were to remember the days when men were rulers; they were to distrust their teachers, and especially the priestesses; they were to look with loathing upon the inaction to which they were condemned; they were told to ask themselves for what end their limbs were strong if they were to do nothing all their lives; and they were taught how, in the old days, the men did all the work, and were rewarded by marrying young and lovely women. This tract had been circulated from hand to hand, none of the agents in its distribution knowing anything of the plot.

There were others, all turning upon the evils of the times, and all recalling the old days when women sat at home.

'We want,' said the Bishop, 'a pretext,—we want a spark which shall set fire to this mass of discontent.'

That very night there was a stormy debate in the House of Peeresses. The Duchess of Dunstanburgh, whose Ministry was kept in power by nothing but the stern will of their leader, because it had never commanded the confidence or even the respect of the House, came down with a bundle of papers in her hand. They were these very tracts. She read them through, one by one. She informed the House that these tracts had been circulated wholesale: from every town in the country she received intelligence that they had been taken from some girl's hands,—in many cases from the innocent hands of young men. She said that it had been ascertained so far that the tracts were posted from Cambridge; it was believed they were the work of certain mischievous and infidel undergraduates. She had taken the unusual course of instituting a college visitation, so far without effect. Meantime she assured the House that if the author of these tracts could be discovered, no punishment would be too severe to meet the offence.

The Countess of Carlyon rose to reply. She said that no one regretted more than herself the tone of these tracts. At the same time there was, without doubt, ample cause for discontent. The professions were crammed; thousands of learned young women were asking themselves where they were to look for even daily bread. In the homes, the young men, seeing the misery, were, for their part, asking why they should not work, if work of any kind were to be got. To sit at home, and starve in gentility, was a hard thing to do, even by the most patient and religious young man; while for a girl to see the days go by barren and unprofitable, while her beauty withered,—to have no hope of marriage; to see the man she might have loved taken from her—here the Countess faced the Duchess with indignant eyes—taken from her by one old enough to be his grandmother,—surely here was cause enough for discontent! She urged the appointment of a commission for the consideration of grievances; and she urged, further, that the evidence of men, old and young, should be received—especially on two important points: first, whether they really liked a life of inaction; and secondly, whether they really liked marrying their grandmothers. The scene which followed this motion was truly deplorable. The following of Lady Carlyon consisted of all the younger members of the House—a minority, but full of life and vigour; on the opposite side were the old and middle-aged Peeresses, who had been brought up in the doctrine of woman's divine right of authority, and of man's divine rule of obedience. The elders had a tremendous majority, of course; but not the less, the fact that such a motion could be made was disquieting. The debate was not reported, but it got abroad; and while the tracts circulated more widely than ever, no more were seized, because they were all kept hidden, and circulated underhand.

From end to end of the country, the talk was of nothing but of the old times. Was it true, the girls asked, that formerly the women ruled at home, while the men did all the work? If that was so, would no one find a compromise by which they could restore that part, at least, of the former régime? Oh, to end these weary struggles,—these studies, which led to examinations; these examinations, which led to diplomas; these diplomas which led to nothing; these agonising endeavours to trample upon each other, to push themselves into notoriety, to snatch the scraps of work from each other's hands! Oh, to rest, to lie still, to watch the men work! Oh—but this they whispered with clasping of hands—oh, to be worshipped by a lover young and loyal! What did the tract say? Happy women of old, when there was no Perfect Woman, but each was the goddess of one man!

CHAPTER X. THE FIRST SPARK

IN the early autumn the Cambridge party broke up. Clarence Veysey was the first to go. His sisters wanted him at home, they said.

'They are good girls,' he sighed, 'and less unsexed than most of their sex. Thanks to my reputation for ill health, they do not interfere with my pursuits, and I can read and meditate. Writing is, of course, dangerous.'

Lord Chester had not been long at the Professor's before he discovered two of those open secrets which are known by everybody. They were naturally affairs of the heart. It was pleasant to find that the young priest, the ardent apostle of the old Faith, was in love, and with Grace Ingleby. The courtship was cold, yet serious; he loved her with the selfish affection of men who have but one absorbing interest in life, and yet want a wife in whom to confide, and from whom to receive undivided care and worship. This he would find in Grace Ingleby,—one of those fond and faithful women who are born full of natural religion, to whom love, faith, and enthusiasm are as the air which they breathe.

The other passion was of a less spiritual kind. Algy Dunquerque, in fact, was in love with Faith Ingleby,—head over ears in love, madly in love,—and she with him. He would break off the most absorbing conversation—even a speculative discussion as to how they would carry themselves, and what they would say, when riding in the cart to execution—in order to walk about under the trees with the girl.

'The fact is,' he explained, 'that if it were not for Faith and for you, I doubt if I should have been secured at all for the Revolution. One more good head would have been saved.'

Another complication made his case serious, and added fresh reasons for despatch in the work before them. His mother addressed him, while he was at Cambridge, a long and serious letter—that kind of letter which must be attended to.

After compliments of the usual kind to the Professor and to Lord Chester,—- it was for the sake of this young man's friendship, and its possible social advantages, that Algy, as well as Jack

Kennion, was permitted to stay so long from home,—Lady Dunquerque opened upon business of a startling nature. She reminded her son that he was now two-and-twenty years of age, a time when many young men of position are already established. 'I have been willing,' she said, 'to give you a long run of freedom,—partly, I confess, because of your friendship for Lord Chester, who, though in many respects not quite the model for quiet and home-loving boys'—here Algy read the passage over again, and nodded his head in approbation—'will be quite certainly the Duke of Dunstanburgh, and in that position will be the first gentleman of England. But an event has occurred, an event of such good fortune, that I am compelled to recall you without delay. You have frequently met the great lawyer Frederica Roe, Q.C. You will, I am sure, be pleased to learn'—here Algy took the hand of Faith Ingleby, and held it, reading aloud—'that she has asked for your hand.'

'I am greatly pleased,' said Algy. 'Bless the dear creature! She dresses in parchment, Faith, my angel: if you prick her, she bleeds ink; if she talks, it is Acts of Parliament; and when she coughs, it is a special pleading. Her complexion is yellow, her eyes are invisible, she has gone bald, and she is five-and-fifty. What good fortune! What blessed luck!' Then he went on with his letter.

'Of course I hastened to accept. She will be raised to the Peerage whenever a vacancy occurs on the Bench. I confess, my dear son, that this match, so much beyond our reasonable expectations, so much higher than our fortune and position entitled us to hope for on your behalf—a match in all respects, and from every point of view, so advantageous—pleases your father and myself extremely. The disparity of age is not greater than many young men have to encounter, and it is proved by numberless examples to be no bar to real happiness. I say this because, in the society of Lord Chester, you may have imbibed—although I rely upon your religious principles—some of those pernicious doctrines which are, falsely perhaps, attributed to him. However, we hope to see you return to us as you left us, submissive, docile, and obedient. And your friendship with Lord Chester may ultimately prove of the greatest advantage to you,' 'I hope it will,' said Jack, laughing, as he read this passage. 'Your father begs me to add that Frederica, who is only a few years older than himself, is in reality, though somewhat imperious and brusque in manner, a most kind-hearted woman, and likely to prove the most affectionate and indulgent of wives.'

'What do you think of that, brothers mine?' he asked, folding up the letter. They looked at each other.

'Oh, begin at once!' cried Faith, clasping her hands. 'They will marry you all, the horrid creatures, before you have struck the first blow. Do you hear, Algy? begin at once.'

'It is serious,' said Jack. 'If pity is any good to you, Algy, you have it. A crabbed old lawyer—a soured, peevish, argumentative Q.C.' He shuddered. 'It is already Vacation; she is sure to want to push on the marriage without delay. What are we to do?'

He looked at Lord Chester for a reply.

'My own case,' said the young Chief, 'comes before the House in October. The first blow, so far as I am concerned, must be struck before then.'

'For Heaven's sake,' cried Algy, 'strike it before this old lawyer swallows me up! I feel like a piece of parchment already. A little delay I can manage; a toothache, a cold, a sore throat—anything would do—but that would only delay the thing a week.'

The little party was broken up. Jack Kennion alone remained. He had obtained permission to accompany Lord Chester to Chester Towers, his country seat. The Professor and the girls were to go too—an arrangement sanctioned by Lady Boltons, happily ordered abroad to drink the waters. Three weeks passed. Letter after letter came from Algy. His fiancée was pressing on the marriage; he had resorted to every expedient to postpone it; he knew not what he could do next;

the day had to be named; wedding presents were coming in; and the learned lawyer proved more odious than could be imagined.

Lord Chester was not idle.

He was sitting one afternoon at this time, Algernon's last despairing letter in his pocket, on a hill-side four or five miles from the Castle. Beside him stood a young gamekeeper, Harry Gilpin, stalwart and brawny: there was no shooting to be done, but he carried his gun.

'It is our only chance, Harry,' said Lord Chester, in low, earnest tones. 'We must do it. Things are intolerable.'

'If there's any chance in it; but it is a poor chance at best.'

'What, Harry! would you not follow me?'

'I'll follow your lordship wherever you lead. I'll go for your lordship wherever you point. Don't think I'm afeard for myself. I'm but a poor creature—easy to find plenty as good as me; and if so be I must end my days in a convict-prison, why, I'd rather do it for you, my lord, than for lying accusations.'

'Good, Harry,' Lord Chester held out his hand. 'We understand each other. Death rather than a convict-prison. We strike for freedom. Tell me next about the discontent.'

'All the country-side is discontented, along o' the old women. It's this way, my lord. We get on right well, let us marry our own gells. When the gells gets shoved out o' the way, and we be told by the Passon to marry this old woman, an' that, why ... 'tis nature.'

'It is, Harry, and my case as well as yours. Then if all are discontented, we may get all to join us.'

'Nay, my lord; many are but soft creatures, and mortal afraid of the women. We shall get some, but we must make them desperate afore they'll fight.'

'You keepers can shoot. How many can we reckon on?'

Harry laughed.

'When your lordship lifts up your little finger,' he replied, 'there's not a keeper for miles and miles round that won't run to join you, nor a stable-boy, nor a groom, nor a gardener. Ay! a hundred and fifty men, counting boys, will come in, once pass the word. A Chester has lived in these parts longer than men can remember.'

'Do they remember, Harry, that a Chester once ruled this country?'

'Ay ... so some say ... in the days when ... but there! it is an old story.'

'But the girls, Harry, who have lost their lovers,—your own girl, what will she do?'

'They whimper a bit; they have a row with the old woman; and then the Passon steps in and talks about religion, and they give in.'

'What! If they saw a chance, if they thought they could get their sweethearts back again, would they not rejoice?'

Harry hesitated.

'Some would, some wouldn't. You see, my lord, it's their religion stands in the way; and their religion means everything. What they say is, that if they married their sweethearts, these being young and proper men, and masterful, they would perhaps get put upon; whereas, they love to rule their husbands. But some would ... yes, some would.'

Lord Chester rose, and began slowly to return home across the fields.

A hundred and fifty, and all true and loyal men! As the occupation of most of them prevented their going to church, and kept them apart from the rest, in a kind of loneliness, they were comparatively uninfluenced by religion; and though their wives drew the pay, the keepers understood little about obedience, and indeed had everything their own way. A hundred and fifty

men!—a little army. Never before had he felt so grateful for the preservation of game.
'You said, Harry, a hundred and fifty men!'
'A hundred and fifty men, my lord, of all ages, by to-morrow morning, if you want them, and no doubt a hundred and fifty more the day after. Why, there are seventy men on the Duchess's estate alone, counting the rangers, the gardeners, the keepers, stable-boys, and all.'
Three hundred men!
Lord Chester was silent. He had communicated enough of the plot. Harry knew that his master, like himself, was threatened with an elderly wife. He also knew that his master proposed an insurrection against the marriage of young men against their wills. Further, Harry did not inquire. Now, while the leader of the Revolt was considering what steps to take,—nothing is harder in revolutions than to make a creditable and startling commencement,—accident put in his way a most excellent beginning. There was a hard-working young blacksmith in the village—a brawny, powerful man of thirty or thereabouts. No better blacksmith was there within thirty miles: his anvil rang from morning until night; he was as handsome in a rough fashion as any man need be; and he ought to have been happy. But he was not, for he was married to a termagant. Not only did this wife of his take all his money, which was legitimate, but she abused him with the foulest reproaches, accusing him perpetually of wife-beating, of infidelity, of drunkenness, and of all the vices to which male flesh is liable, threatening him in her violent moods with imprisonment.
That morning there had been a more than usually violent quarrel. The scolding of the beldam in her house was heard over the whole village, so that the men trembled and grew pale, thus admonished of what an angry woman can say. During the forenoon there was peace, the blacksmith working quietly at his forge. In the dinner-hour the row began again, worse than ever. At two o'clock the poor man came out with hanging head and dejected face to his work. One or two of the elder women admonished him against exasperating his wife; but he replied nothing. Children, for whom the unlucky smith had ever a kind word and a story, came as usual, and stayed outside waiting. But there was no word of kindness for them that day. Men passed down the village street and spoke to him; but he made no reply. Then the village cobbler, a widower, and independent, and so old and crusty of temper that no one was likely to marry him, came forth from his shop and spoke to him.
'How goes it, Tom?'
'Bad,' said Tom. 'Couldn't be worse. And I wish I was dead—dead and buried and out of it.'
The cobbler shook his head and retired.
Then there came slowly down the street, carrying a basket with vegetables, a young woman of five-and-twenty, and she stopped in front of the forge, and said softly, 'Poor Tom! I heard her this morning.'
Tom looked up and shook his head. His eyes, which were soft and gentle, were full of tears.
And then ... then ... the wife rushed upon the scene. Her eyes were red, her lips were quivering, her whole frame shook with passion. For she was no longer simply in a common, vulgar, everyday rage; she was in a rage of jealousy. She seized the younger woman by the arm, dragged her into the middle of the road, and threw herself before her husband in a fine attitude. 'Stand back!' she cried. 'You ... you ... Susan! He is my man, not yours—not yours.'
'Poor fellow!' said Susan. She was a young person with black hair and resolute eyes, and it was well known that she had regarded Tom as her sweetheart. 'Poor fellow! It was a bad job indeed for him when he became your man.'
. . . .
A war of words between an elderly woman, who may be taunted with her years, her jealousy, her

lack of children, teeth, and comeliness, and a young woman, who may be charged with many sins, is at best a painful thing to witness, and a shameful thing to describe. Suffice it to say, that the elder lady was completely discomfited, and that long after she was extinguished, the girl continued to pour upon her the vials of her wrath. The whole village meanwhile—all the women, and such of the men as were too old for work—crowded round, taking part in the contest.

Finally, the wife, stung by words whose bitterness was embittered by their truth, cried aloud, taking the bystanders to witness, that the husband for whose sake, she said, she had endured patiently the falsehoods and accusations of yonder hussy, was nothing better than a beater, a striker, a kicker, a trampler, and a cuffer of his wife.

'I've borne it long,' she cried, 'but I will bear it no longer. To prison he shall go. If I am an old woman, and like to die, you shall never have him—do you hear? To prison he shall go, and for life.'

At these words a dead silence fell on all.

The blacksmith stood still, saying not a word, leaning on his hammer. Then his wife spoke again, but slowly.

'Last night,' she said, 'he dragged me round the room by the hair of my head; this morning he knocked me down with his fist; and last Sunday, after church, he kicked me off my chair; yesterday fortnight he beat me with a poker——'

'Lies! lies!! LIES!!!' cried Susan. 'Tom say they are lies.'

Tom shook his head but spoke never a word.

'Tom!' she cried again, 'they will take you to prison; say they are lies.'

Then he spoke.

'I would rather go to prison.'

'Don't believe her,' Susan cried. 'Don't believe her. Why, she's got no hair to be pulled.... Don't ... Oh! oh! oh!'

She burst into an agony of weeping.

The women clamoured round the group,—some for justice, because wife-beating is an awful sin; some for mercy, because this woman was in her fits of wrath a most notorious liar, and not a soul believed her accusations.

It was in the midst of this altercation that there arrived on the scene, from opposite points, Lord Chester with Harry, and two of the rural police.

'Take him into custody,' gasped the blacksmith's wife. 'Take him to prison. Oh, the wretch! oh, the wife-beater! oh, I am beaten to a jelly—I am bruised black and blue!'

Lord Chester stepped before the unhappy blacksmith.

'Stay!' he said to the policewomen. 'Not so fast. Tom, what do you say?' he asked the blacksmith.

'I never laid hand on her,' said the unhappy man. 'But all's one for that. I suppose I'll have to go to prison, my lord. Anyhow, there can't be no prison worse than this life. I'm glad and happy to be rid of her.'

'Stay again,' said his lordship. The people gathered closer in wonder. The masterful young lord looked as if he meant to interfere. 'Some of you,' he said, 'take this woman away, and look for any marks of violence. No,' as the elder women pressed forward, 'not you who have got young husbands of your own, and would like to get rid of them yourselves perhaps. Some of you girls take her.'

But she refused to go, while the old women murmured amongst each other.

'Must obey orders, my lord,' said one of the police. 'Here's a case for the magistrates. Woman

says her husband struck, beat, and kicked her. Magistrates will hear the case, my lord.'
She pulled out her handcuffs.
Then Lord Chester saw that the moment had arrived.
'Harry,' he said, 'stand by.'
He laid his hand on the blacksmith's shoulder.
'No one shall harm him,' he said. 'Tom, come with me.'
'My lord!... my lord!' cried the policewomen. 'What shall we do? It's obstructing law—it's threatening the executive: what will the justices say? It's a most dreadful offence.'
'Come, Tom,' he said.
The crowd parted right and left with awestruck eyes.
As Lord Chester carried off his rescued prisoner, the Vicar came running out with dismay upon her face.
'My lord! my lord!' she cried. 'What dreadful thing is this? And you, Tom,—you, after all your promises! In my parish, too!'
'Hold your foolish tongue!' said Lord Chester, roughly. 'Why not in your parish? In every parish, thanks to you and your accursed religion, the young men are torn from the girls, and there is misery. Stand aside.... You, Susan, will you come with me and your old sweetheart?'
The Vicar gasped. She turned white with terror. 'Foolish tongue! Accursed religion!' Had she heard aright?
The police-constables looked stupidly at one another.
'Please, my lord,' said one, 'we must report your lordship.'
'Go and report,' replied the rebel.
It was now half-past five in the afternoon, and the labourers were returning from the fields. The village street was crowded with men, most of them young men.
The men began whispering together, and the women were all delivering orations at once.
The Chief pointed to some of the men and called them by name.
'You, John Deer; you, Nick Trulliber; you—and you—and you,—come with me. You have old wives too; unless you want to be sent to prison for life for wife-beating, come with me and fight for your liberty.'
They hesitated; they trembled; they looked at the vicar, at their wives: they would have been lost but for the presence of mind of the cobbler.
He was, as I have said, an elderly man, bowed down by his work and by years. But he sprang to the front and shouted to the men:—
'Come, unless you are cowards and deserve the hulks. Why, it's slavery, it's misery; it's unnatural pains and penalties. Come out of it, you poor, wretched chaps, that ought to be married to them as is young and comely. Come away, all you young fellows that want young wives. Hooray! his lordship's going to deliver us all. Three cheers for Lord Chester! We'll fight for our liberty.'
He brandished his bradawl, seized one of the men, and the rest followed. There was a general scream from the women of rage and terror; for all the men followed, like sheep, in a body. Not a single man of the village under sixty years of age or over sixteen slept in his wife's house that night.
'I always knew, my lord,' said the cobbler, 'that it was stuff an' nonsense, them and their submission. Yah! some day there was bound to be a row. Don't let 'em go back, my lord. I'll stick by your lordship.'
('It is a very odd thing,' said the Professor, when she heard the story, 'that cobblers have always

been atheists.')

What next?

Lord Chester had now got his men—a band forty-seven strong, nearly all farm-labourers—within the iron gates of his park, and these were closed and locked. They were as fine a body of men, both young and old together, as could be collected anywhere. But they understood as yet nothing of what was going to be done, and they slouched along wondering stupidly, yet excited at the risk they were running.

Lord Chester made them a speech.

'Remember,' he said, 'that the prisons of England are full of men charged with wife-beating. They never had an opportunity of defending themselves; they are tortured day and night. You may, all of you—any of you—be charged with this offence. Your word is not taken; you are carried off to hopeless imprisonment. Is that a pleasant thing for you?'

They murmured. But Tom the blacksmith waved his hammer, and Harry the keeper his gun, and the cobbler his bradawl, and these three shouted.

'Who asked you,' cried Lord Chester, 'if you wanted to marry an old woman? Did any of you choose her for yourselves? Why, when there were girls in the village, sweet and young and pretty, longing for your love, is it likely you would take an old woman?'

Then the girl they called Susan, who had followed with Tom, sprang to the front.

'Look at me, all of you,' she cried. 'Tom and me was courtin' since we were children—wasn't we, Tom.' Tom nodded assent. 'And she comes and takes him from me. And the Passon said it was all right, because a man must obey, and sweetheartin' was nonsense. How long are you going to stand it? If I was a man, and strong, would I let the women have their own way? How long will you stand it, I say?'

Here the men lifted up their voices and growled. Liberty begins with a growl; rage begins with a growl; fighting begins with a growl,—it is a healthy symptom for those who promote mischief.

'Are they pretty, your old women?' the orator went on. 'Are they good-tempered? Are they pleasant to live with?'

There was another growl.

'Men,' cried Lord Chester, 'we have borne enough. Wake up! We will end all this. We will marry the women we love—the pretty sweethearts who love us—the young girls who will make us happy. Who will follow us?'

Harry the keeper stepped to the front with a shout. Tom the blacksmith followed with a shout, brandishing his hammer. The cobbler pushed and shoved the men. Susan threw her arms round Tom's neck and kissed him, crying, 'Go and fight, Tom; follow his lordship. Come, all you that are not cowards.'

Two things happened then which determined the event and rallied the waverers, who, to tell the truth, were already beginning to expect their wives and sisters upon the scene.

The first was the appearance of Jack Kennion, followed by two men bearing a great cask of beer. Then tankards passed from lip to lip, and the courage which is said to belong to Holland rather than to England mounted in their hearts.

'Drink about, lads,' cried Jack. 'Here! give me the mug. Hurrah for Lord Chester! Drink about. Hurrah!'

They drank—they shouted. And while they shouted they became aware of a tall and beautiful girl who came from the house and stood beside Lord Chester. Her lips were parted; her long hair flowed upon her shoulders; the tears stood in her beautiful eyes. She tried to speak, but for a moment could not.

'Oh, men!' she cried at last,—'Men of England! I thank kind Heaven for this day, which is the beginning of your freedom. Oh, be brave! think not of your own wrongs only. Think of the thousands of men lingering in prison; think of all who are shut in houses, working all day for their unloved wives; think of the young girls who have lost their lovers; think of your strength and your courage, and fight—to the death, if needs be!'

'We will fight,' cried the cobbler, 'to the death!'

Then Grace Ingleby, for it was she, went from man to man and from group to group, praising them, telling them that it was no small thing they had done—that no common or cowardly man would have dared to do it; commending their courage, admiring their strength, and informing them carefully that this their act could never be forgiven, so that if they did not succeed they would assuredly all be hanged; and imploring them to lose no time in drilling and learning the use of weapons.

The Professor, meantime, was writing letters. She wrote to her husband, begging him to remain quiet while the news was spreading abroad, when he had better get across country by night and join the insurgents. She wrote to all the disciples, telling them to escape and make their way to Lord Chester; and assisted by the girls of the household, who all espoused the cause of the men, she took down the guns, swords, and weapons from the walls, and brought them out for use.

After supper—they cooked plentiful chops for the hungry men, with more beer—Jack called the men out for first drill. It was hard work; but then drill cannot at first be anything but hard work. The men were armed with pikes, guns, clubs, anything; and before nightfall, they had received their first lesson in the art of standing shoulder by shoulder.

They slept that night in tents made of sheets spread out on sticks—a rough shelter, but enough. But the chiefs sat till late, thinking and talking.

Early in the morning, at daybreak, Lord Chester dropped asleep, worn out. When he awoke, Grace stood over him with smiling face.

'Come, my lord,' she said, 'I have something to show you.'

He stood upon the terrace. The night before, he had seen a group of fellows in smock-frocks shoving each other about in a vain attempt to stand in rank and file. Now, the lawns were crowded with men of a different kind, who had come in during the night.

First and foremost, there were a hundred bronzed and weather-beaten men armed with guns—they were Harry's friends, the keepers, rangers, and foresters; among them stood a score of boys who had been sent round to summon them; and behind the keepers stood the rustics.

Oh, wonderful conversion! They had been already put into some sort of uniform which was found among the lumber of the Castle. The jackets were rusty of colour and moth-eaten, but they made the men look soldier-like; every man had round his arm a scarlet ribbon; some had scarlet coats, but not many. At sight of their Chief they all shouted together and brandished their weapons.

The Revolt of Man had begun!

CHAPTER XI. A MARRIAGE MARRED

THERE was great excitement in the village of Much cum Milton—a little place about thirty miles from Chester Towers—because Lady Dunquerque's only son, Algernon, was to be married that day to the great lawyer, Frederica Roe. Apart from the natural joy with which such an event is welcomed in a monotonous country village, Algernon was deservedly popular. No better rider, no better shot, no stouter, handsomer lad was to be found in the country-side; nor was it to his discredit that he was the personal friend of young Lord Chester, whose Case was on everybody's lips; nor, among young people, was it to his discredit that he was suspected of being on Lady Carlyon's side. The village girls smiled and looked meaningly at each other when he passed: there were reports that the young man had more than once shown a certain disposition to freedoms; but these, for the sake of his father's feelings, were not spread abroad; and indeed, in country districts, things which would have ruined a young man's reputation in town—such as kissing a dairymaid or a dressmaker—were rather regarded with favour by the girls thus outraged.

The only drawback to the general joy was the thought that the bride was over fifty years of age. Even making great allowances for the safety which experience gives, it is not often that a young man who has attracted the affections of a woman thirty years his senior, is found to study how to preserve those affections; and even considering the position offered by a woman safe of the next vacancy among the judges, a difference of thirty years did seem to these village girls, who knew little of the ways of the great world, a bar to true love. Their opinion, however, was not asked, and the festivities were not outwardly marred by them.

Early in the morning the village choir assembled on the lawn beneath the bridegroom's chamber, and sang the well-known wedding-hymn beginning:—

Break, happy day! Rise, happy sun!
Breathe softer, airs of Paradise!
The days of hope and doubt are done;
To higher heights of love we rise.
Ah! trembling heart of trusting youth,
Fly to the home of peace and rest;
From woman's hands receive the truth,
In woman's arms be fully blessed.
O sweet exchange! O guerdon strange!
For love and guidance of a wife,
To yield the will, and follow still
In holy meekness all your life.

The bridegroom-elect within his room made no sign; the window-blind was not disturbed. As a matter of fact, Algy was half-dressed, and was sitting in a chair looking horribly ill at ease.

They began to ring the bells at six; by eight the whole village population was out upon the Green, and the final preparations were made. Of course there were Venetian masts, with gay-coloured flags flying. The tables were spread in a great marquee for the feast which, at mid-day, was to be given to the whole village. There were to be sports and athletics for the young men on the Green; there was to be dancing in the evening; there was a band already beginning to discourse sweet music; there was a circus, which was to perform twice, and both times for nothing; there were ginger-bread booths, and rifle-galleries, and gipsies to tell fortunes; they had set up the perambulating theatre for the drama of Punch and Judy, in which the reprobate Punch, who dares to threaten his wife with violence, and disobeys her orders, is hanged upon the stage—a moral lesson of the greatest value to boys; and there was a conjuring-woman's tent. The church was gaily dressed with flowers, and all the boys of the village were told off to strew roses, though the season was late, under the feet of bride and bridegroom.

At the Hall an early breakfast was spread; but the young bridegroom, the hero of the day, was late.

'Poor boy,' said his sister, 'no doubt he is anxious and excited with so much happiness before him.'

It was a well-bred family, and the disparity of age was not allowed to be even hinted at. The marriage was to be considered a love-match on both sides: that was the social fiction, though everybody knew what was said and thought. Lady Dunquerque had got the boy off her hands very well: there was an excellent establishment, and a good position, with a better one to follow; as for love—here girls looked at each other and smiled. Love was become a thing no longer possible, except for heiresses, of whom there are never too many. Fifty years of age and more; a harsh voice, a hard face, a hard manner, an unsympathetic, exact woman, wrinkled and gray-haired,—how, in the name of outraged Cupid, could such a woman be loved by such a lad? But these things were not even spoken,—they were only conveyed to each other by looks, and smiles, and nods, and little movements of the hands.

'I think, Robert,' said Lady Dunquerque, 'that you had better go up and call Algernon.' Sir Robert obediently rose and departed.

When he came down again, his face, usually as placid as the face of a sheep, was troubled. 'Algernon will not take any breakfast,' he said.

'Nonsense! the boy must take breakfast. Is he dressed?' Lady Dunquerque was evidently not disposed to surrender her authority over her son till he had actually passed into the hands of his wife.

'Yes, yes,—he is nearly dressed,' stammered her husband.

'Well, then, go and tell him to come to breakfast at once, without any nonsense.'

Sir Robert went once more. Again he came back with the intelligence that the boy refused to come down.

Thereupon Lady Dunquerque herself went up to his room. The two girls looked at each other with apprehension. Algy was hot-headed: he had already, though not before his mother, made use of very strong language about his bride; could he be meditating some disobedience? Horrible! And the guests all invited, and the day arrived, and the boy's wedding outfit actually ready!

'What did he say, papa?' one of them asked.

I cannot tell you, my dear. I wash my hands of it. Your mother must bring him to reason. I have done my best.' Sir Robert answered in a nervous trembling manner not usual with him.

'Does he ... does he ... express any unwillingness?' asked his daughter.

'My dear, he says nothing shall make him marry the lady. That is all. The day arrived and everything. No power on earth, he says, shall make him marry the lady. That is all. What will come to us if her ladyship cannot make him hear reason, I dare not think.'

Just then Lady Dunquerque returned. Her husband, trembling visibly, dared not lift his eyes.

'My dear girls,' she said, with the calmness of despair, 'we are disgraced for ever. The boy refuses to move. He disregards threats entreaties, everything. I have appealed to his obedience, to his religion, to his honour—all is of no avail. Go yourselves, if you can. Now, Sir Robert, if you have anything to advise, let me hear it.'

'I can advise nothing,' said her husband, quite overwhelmed with this misfortune. 'Who could have thought that a——'

'Yes—yes,—it is of no use lamenting. What are we to do? Heavens! there are the church bells again!'

Meantime his sisters were with Algernon. They found him sitting grim and determined. Never before had they seen that expression of determination upon a man's face. He absolutely terrified them.

'You are come to try your powers, I suppose?' he said. 'Well; have your say. But remember, no power on earth shall make me marry that detestable old woman.'

'Algernon!' cried his younger sister. 'Is it possible that you ... you ... our own brother, should use these words?'

'A great deal more is possible. I, for one, protest against this abominable sale of men in marriage. I am put up in the market; this rich old lawyer, with a skin of parchment, blood of ink, heart of brown paper, buys me: I will not be bought. Go, tell my mother that she may do her worst. I will not marry the woman.'

'If you will not think of yourself,' said his elder sister coldly, 'pray think of us. Our guests are invited,—they are already assembling in the church; listen—there are the bells!'

'I should like,' said Algy laughing,—'I should like to see the face of Frederica Roe in half an hour's time.'

The two girls looked at each other in dismay. What was to be done? what could be said?

'You two little hypocrites!' he went on. 'you and your goody talk about the day of happiness! and the humbugging hymn! and your sham and mockery of the Perfect Woman! and your reign of the Intellect! Wait a little, my sisters; I promise you a pleasing change in the monotony of your lives.'

'Sister,' said the younger, 'he blasphemes. We must leave him. Oh, unhappy boy! what fate are you preparing for yourself?'

'Come,' answered the elder. 'Come away, my dear. Algernon, if you disgrace us this day, you shall be no more brother of mine; I renounce you.'

They left him. Presently his father came back.

'Algernon,' he said feebly, 'have you come to your right mind?'

'I have,' he replied—'I have. That is the reason why I am here, and why I am staying here.'

'Then I can do nothing for you. Poor boy! my heart bleeds for you.'

'My poor father,' said his son, speaking in a parable, 'my heart has bled for you a long time. Patience!—wait a little.'

'The last wedding-present has arrived,' said Sir Robert. 'What we are to do I cannot, dare not, think. Your mother must break the news to Frederica.'

'Whose is the wedding-present?'

'It is from Lord Chester—the most magnificent hunter, saddled, and all; with a note.'

Algernon sprang to his feet and rushed to the window. On the carriage-drive he saw a little stable-boy leading a horse. He knew the boy as one of Lord Chester's—a sharp, trusty lad. What was the horse saddled for?

'Give me the letter,' he said almost fiercely, to his father.

Sir Robert handed him the note, which lady Dunquerque had opened and read:—

'Congratulations, dear Algy; the happy day has dawned.—Yours most sincerely,

'Chester.'

'Among other disasters, you will lose this friend, Algy,' moaned his father. 'No one can ever speak to you again; no one can——'

'Tell my mother, sir, that I am ready,' he interrupted, with a most extraordinary change of manner. 'I will be with her as soon as I can complete my toilet. One must be smart upon one's wedding-day. Go, dear father, tell her I am coming downstairs, and beg her not to make a row—I mean, not to allude to the late distressing scene.'

He pushed his father out of the room.

Two minutes later he stood in the breakfast-room, actually laughing as if nothing had happened.

'I am glad my son,' said his mother, 'that you have returned to your senses.'

'Yes,' he replied gaily, as if it had been a question of some simple act of petulance; 'it is a good thing, isn't it? Have you seen Lord Chester's gift, sisters?'
The girls looked at each other in a kind of stupor. What could men be like that they should so lightly pass from one extreme to the other?
'Tell the boy,' he ordered the footman, 'to lead the horse to the Green; I should like all the lads to see it. Tell them it is Lord Chester's gift, with his congratulations on the dawn of the happy day—tell them to remember the dawn of the happy day.'
He seemed to talk nonsense in his excitement. But Sir Robert, overjoyed at this sudden return to obedience, shed tears.
'Now,' said Lady Dunquerque, 'we have no time to lose. Girls, you can go on with your father. Algernon, of course, accompanies me.'
When they were left alone, his mother began a lecture, short but sharp, on the duty of marital obedience.
'I say no more,' she concluded,' on the lamentable display of temper of this morning. Under the circumstances, I pass it over on condition that you look your brightest and best all day, and that you show yourself alive to the happiness of the position I have gained for you.'
'I think,' he replied, 'that in the future, if not to-day, you will congratulate yourself on my line of action.'
A strange thing for the young man to say. Afterwards they remembered it, and understood it.
Meantime the churchyard was full of the village people, and the church was crammed with the guests in wedding-favours; on the Green the band was discoursing sweet music; in the centre, an object of the deepest admiration for the village lads, stood Lord Chester's gift, led by his boy.
At a quarter to eleven punctually, the carriage containing the bride and principal bridesmaid, a lady also of the Inner Bar, about her own age, arrived. The bride was beautifully dressed in a rich white satin. She was met in the porch by the other bridesmaids, including the groom's sisters. All were in great spirits, and even the harsh face of the bride looked smiling and kind. The sisters, reassured on the score of their brother, were rejoicing in the sunshine of the day, the crowds, and the general joy. Sir Robert and the other elderly gentlemen were standing in meditation, or devoutly kneeling before the chancel.
Hush! silence! Hats off in the churchyard! There are the wheels of the bridegroom's carriage. Here come the Vicar and the Choir ready to strike up the Processional Hymn. Clash, clang the bells! one more, and altogether, if it brings down the steeple! Now the lads make a lane outside. Off hats! Cheer with a will, boys! Hurrah for the bridegroom! He sits beside his mother, his head back, his eyes flashing; he laughs a greeting to the crowd.
'Capital, Algernon!' says his mother. 'Now subdue your joy; we are at the lych-gate.'
The carriage stopped. Algernon sprang out, and assisted his mother to alight. Then the procession, already formed, began slowly to move up the aisle singing the hymn, and the notes of the organ rolled among the old low arches of the little village church; and the Vicar walked last, carrying her hymn-book in her hand, singing lustily, and thinking, poor woman, that the marriage procession was advancing behind her.
Well, it was not; and when she turned round, having reached the altar, she stared blankly, because there was no marriage procession, but a general looking at each other, and whispering. What happened was this.
After helping Lady Dunquerque out of the carriage, Algernon quietly left her, and without the slightest appearance of hurry, calmly walked across the Green and mounted Lord Chester's gift. Then he rode to the churchyard gate, and took off his hat to his bride, and shouted, so that all

could hear him, even in the church, 'Very sorry, old lady, but you must look for another husband.' Then he turned his horse and cantered quickly away through the crowd, laughing and waving his hand.

Half an hour later, Frederica Roe, after a stormy scene with Lady Dunquerque, which ended in the latter thanking Providence for having delivered her headstrong boy, even at the last moment, from so awful a temper, returned with her best-maid to town. There was laughter that evening when the news reached the Club. Cruel things, too, were said by the Juniors. There would have been more cruel things but for the circumstances which followed.

It was naturally a day of Rebuke at the village. The circus, the gipsies, the conjurors, and the acrobats, were all packed off about their business; there was no feast; the children were sent back to school; the wedding-guests dispersed in dismay; and Lady Dunquerque, with rage and despair in her heart, sat amid her terror-stricken household, none daring to say a word to soothe and comfort her. Later on, her husband suggested the consolations of religion, but these failed.

The summons reached Clarence Veysey on the next day. The boy who brought him the letter had ridden fifty miles.

He was waiting at home in great despondency. The perpetual acting, the deception, tortured his earnest soul; he lacked companionship; he wanted the conversation of Grace Ingleby; his sisters wearied him with their talk, and their aims—aims which he was about to make impossible for them. The boy, who was the son of one of Lord Chester's keepers, came to the house by the garden entrance, and found Clarence walking on the lawn. He tore open the note, which was as follows:—

'Come at once; we have begun.—C.'

Then Clarence waited for nothing, but started to walk to Chester Towers. He walked for four-and-twenty hours; when he arrived he was faint with hunger and fatigue, but he was there. The Rebellion had begun, and he was with the rebels.

CHAPTER XII. IN THE CAMP AT CHESTER TOWERS

THE first days were spent in drill, in exhortation, in feasting, and in singing. Grace Ingleby fitted new words to old tunes, and the men sang them marching across the park. A detachment of keepers was placed at the gates to receive new recruits, and to keep out the women who crowded round them all day long—some laughing, some crying, some threatening. The women of the Castle, being offered their choice whether to remain in the service of the Earl or to go at once, divided themselves into two parties—the elder women deciding to go, and the younger to remain; 'for,' as they said, 'if the men ride all over the country, as Mrs Ingleby says they will, what can we women do to keep them down?' And then they blamed the unequal marriages, and irreligious things were said about the Duchess of Dunstanburgh. Those who stayed were employed in making rosettes and ribbons in scarlet silk, and in getting out of the old lumber-rooms all the finery which could be found to serve for the men's uniforms.

'First rule,' said Jack the prudent, 'keep the men's spirits up—with beer, and singing, and feasting; next, make them proud of their gallant show.'

Every hour raised the spirits of the men, every moment new recruits came in, who were greeted with shouts, beer, and exhortation, chiefly from the cobbler, who now wore a glittering helmet, and carried a ten-foot pike.

In the course of the next two or three days all the Bishop's disciples came in: Clarence Veysey, dusty and wayworn, yet full of ardour; Algy Dunquerque rode in gallantly, laughing at his escape. The others came in one after the other, eager for employment, and were at once set to work. No time this for love-making; but Grace exchanged a few words with Clarence, and Faith ran about among the men, telling them all that Captain Dunquerque was her sweetheart, asking who were the girls they loved, and how they wooed them, and so delightfully turning everything upside down that she was better than all the barrels of beer.

Lord Chester was the Chief, but Captain Dunquerque was the favourite. It was he who kept everybody in good spirits—who organised races in the evening, set the men to box, to wrestle, to fight with single-stick, with prizes and cheering for the winners; so that the lads for the first time in their lives felt the fierce joy of battle and the pride of victory. It was Captain Dunquerque who had a word for every man, forgetting none of their names; who praised them and encouraged them, was all day long in the camp, never tired, never lost his temper—as some of the keepers did who were promoted to be sergeants; who was generous with the beer; who promised to every man money, independent work, and a pretty wife—after the Cause was won. So that Algy Dunquerque, the first commander-in-chief under the new régime, began his popularity as the soldiers' general from the very first.

On the evening of his arrival, Clarence preached to the men—a faithful discourse, which yet only revealed half the Truth. We must destroy before we can build up.

He bade them remember that they were, as men, the workers of the world—nothing could be done except by them; and then he told them some of the wonders which had been accomplished by their forefathers in the days when men had been acknowledged to be the thinkers and creators as well as the workers, and he told them in such simple language as he could command, how, since women had taken over the reins, everything had gone backwards. Lastly, he bade them remember what they were, what their lives had been, how slavish and how sad, and what their lives would still continue to be unless they freed themselves.

'Time was—the good old time—when every man could raise himself, when there was a ladder from the lowest station to the highest. Now, as you are born, so you must die. No rising for you—no hope for you. Work and slave—and die. That is your lot. They invented a religion to keep you down. They told you that it is the will of Heaven that you should obey women. It is a LIE.' The preacher shouted the words. 'It is a LIE. There is no such religion; and I am here to teach you the Truth, when you have proved that you are fit to receive it.'

The preacher was received with an indifference which was discouraging. In fact, the men had been preached at so long, that they had ceased to pay any attention to sermons. Nor could even Clarence's earnestness surpass that of the Preaching Order, the Holy sisterhood, which trained its members in the art of inspiring Hope, Terror, and Faith.

The address finished, the men betook them once more to singing, while the beer went round about their camp-fires. Here was a glorious change! Even the gamekeepers—a race not easily moved—congratulated each other on the recovery of their freedom. That night a proclamation was made in camp that every man would receive his pay himself—the same as that earned in the fields—in full. Men looked at each other and wondered. Those who only half believed in the Cause were reassured. To be paid, instead of seeing your wife paid, proved, as nothing else could, the strength and reality of the Rebellion. Another proclamation was made, repealing all prohibitions for men to assemble, remain out-of-doors after sunset, and form societies. This was even more warmly received than the former proclamation, because many of the men did not know what to do with their money when they got it; whereas they had all of them learned this grand pleasure of companionship, drink, and song.

On that night and the next, two councils were held, big with importance to the Realm of England.

The first of these was at Chester Towers, under the presidency of Lord Chester. There were present the Bishop—whose impatience made him set out on the first receipt of the news—Clarence Veysey, Algernon Dunquerque, Jack Kennion, and the rest of the disciples. The Professor and the girls were in the room but they did not speak.

They sat until late considering many things. Had they known more of man's real nature, there would have been no hesitation, and a bold forward march might have saved many difficulties. The Bishop and Clarence Veysey, who believed the Truth by itself a sufficient weapon, wanted to await the arrival of all Englishmen in the Park, and meantime to be preaching perpetually. Algernon was for movement. The Chief at last decided on a compromise. They would advance, but slowly; and would send out, meanwhile, scouts and small parties to bring in recruits. The danger of the Revolt, provided it were sufficiently widespread, lay chiefly in the imagination. It was difficult even for the leaders, who had been so long and so carefully trained by the Bishop and his wife, to shake off the awe inspired by the feminine oppression and their early training. Every woman seemed still their natural ruler, yet the Reign of Woman rested on no more solid basis than this awe. Its only defence lay in the regiments of Horse Guards and its Convict Wardens; while, to make the latter available, the prisoners would have to be discharged.

The other council of war was held in the House of Peeresses, called together hastily. There had been grave disquiet all day long; and though nothing definite was known, it was whispered that there was an outbreak of the Men. A Cabinet Council was called at noon, the Home Department was agitated, the secretaries went about with pale faces, there was continual ringing of bells and scurrying of clerks, the Archbishop of Canterbury was sent for hurriedly, crowds of women gathered about the lobbies of the House, and it was presently known everywhere that the thing most dreaded of all things had happened—a Rising. Outside the House it was not yet known where this had occurred, nor under what leaders: within, the doors were closed, and in the midst of a silence most profound and most unusual, the Duchess of Dunstanburgh rose, with papers in her hand.

She briefly announced that a rebellion had broken out in Norfolk. A score or so of poor peasants belonging to one small village had risen in revolt. They were headed by Lord Chester. It was nothing—a mere lamentable outbreak, which would be put down at once by the strong hand of law.

Then she sat down. All faces were turned immediately to her Grace's young rival. Lady Carlyon rose and asked if her Grace had any more details to give the House. She implored the Government to put the House in possession of all the facts, however painful they might be. The Duchess replied that the news of this insurrection, about which there could unfortunately be no doubt, reached her that morning only. It arrived in the shape of a Report drawn up by the Vicar of Chester Towers, and sworn before two justices of the peace. The rising, if it was worthy to be called by such a name, was begun by the forcible rescue from the hands of the law of a certain blacksmith—a scoundrel guilty of wife-beating in its most revolting forms. He was torn from the hands of the police by Lord Chester and a gamekeeper. The misguided young man then called upon the men of the village to rise and follow him. He led them to his own Castle. He was joined by a body of gamekeepers, and men connected with manly sports of other kinds. By the last advices, he had gone the desperate length of defying the Government, and was now drilling and arming his troops. The Duchess assured the House again that there was nothing to fear except a probable loss of life, which was lamentable, but must be faced; that the Government had ordered two thousand of the Convict Wardens to be held in readiness, and that meanwhile they had sent two sisters of the Holy Preaching Order with twenty constables to disperse the mob. As for the

ringleaders, they appeared to be, besides Lord Chester himself, Professor Ingleby of Cambridge, her husband, her two daughters, and a band of some half-dozen young gentlemen. The House might rest assured that signal justice would be done upon these mad and wicked people, and that no favour should be shown to rank or sex. As for herself, the House knew the relations which existed between herself and Lord Chester——
Lady Carlyon sprang to her feet, and asked what relations these were. The Duchess went on to say that there was no occasion to dilate upon what was perfectly well known. She would, however, assure the House that this unhappy man had cut himself off altogether from her sympathy. She gave up, without a sigh, hopes that had once been dear to her, and left a miscreant so godless, so abandoned, to his fate.
Lady Carlyon begged the House to suspend its judgment until the facts were clearly known. At present all that appeared certain was, that a body of men had locked themselves within the gates of Lord Chester's park. She would ask her Grace whether any grievances had been stated.
The Duchess replied that at the right moment the alleged grievances, if there were any, would be laid before the House.
Lady Carlyon asked again whether one of the grievances was not the custom—falsely alleged to be based upon religion—which compelled young men to marry women who were unsuitable and distasteful to them by reason of age, temper, or other incompatibility?
This was the signal for the most frightful scene of disorder ever witnessed in the House; for all Peeresses with husbands younger than themselves screamed on one side, and the young Peeresses on the other. After a little quiet had been obtained, Lady Carlyon was heard again, and accused the Duchess of Dunstanburgh of being herself the sole cause of the Insurrection. 'It is time,' she said, 'to use plainness of speech. Let us recognise the truth that a young man cannot but abhor and loathe so unnatural a union as that of twenty years with forty, fifty, sixty. For my own part, I do not wonder that a man so high-spirited as Lord Chester should have been driven to madness. All in this House know well, without any pretences as to the honour of Peeresses, that a majority in favour of the Duchess was certain. Can any one believe that the judgment of the House would have been given for the happiness of the young man? Can any one believe that he could have contemplated the proposed union without repugnance? We know well what the end of the rising may be; and of this am I well assured, that the blood of this unhappy boy, and the blood of all those who perish with him, are upon the head of the Duchess of Dunstanburgh.'
Then began another terrible scene, in which all the invective, the recrimination, the accusations, the insinuations, of which the language is capable, seemed gathered together and hurled at each other: there was no longer a Government and an Opposition; there was the wrath of the young, who had seen, or looked to see, the men they might have loved torn from them by the old; there was the fury of the old, calling upon Religion, Law, Piety, and Order.
Constance withdrew in the height of the battle, having said all she had to say. It was a clear and bright morning; the sun was already rising; there were little groups of women hanging about the lobbies still, waiting for news. One of them stepped forward and saluted Constance. She was a young journalist of great promise, and had often written leaders at Constance's suggestion.
'Has your ladyship any more news?' she asked.
'I know nothing but what I have heard from ... from the Duchess.' It was by an effort that Constance pronounced her name. 'I know no more.'
'We have heard more,' the journalist went on. 'We have heard from Norfolk, by a girl who galloped headlong into town with the intelligence, and is now at the War Office, that, yesterday morning at nine o'clock, Lord Chester rode out of his Park, followed by his army, carrying

banners, and armed with guns, pikes, and swords. They are said to number at present some two or three hundred only.'

Constance was too weary and worn with the night's excitement to receive this dreadful news. She burst into passionate tears.

'Edward,' she cried, 'you rush upon certain death!' Then she recovered herself. 'Stay! let me think. We must do something to allay the excitement. The Government will issue orders to keep the men at home—that is their first thought. We must do more: we must agitate for a reform. There is one concession that must be made. Go at once and write the strongest leader you ever wrote in all your life: treat the rebellion as of the slightest possible importance; do not weigh heavily upon the unhappy Chief; talk as little as possible about misguided lads; say that, without doubt, the men will disperse; urge an amnesty; and then strike boldly and unmistakably for the great grievance of men and women both. Raise the Cry of "The Young for the Young!" And keep harping on this theme from day to day.'

It was, however, too late for newspaper articles: a wild excitement ran through the streets of London; the men were kept indoors; workmen who had to go abroad were ordered not to stop on their way, not to speak with each other, not to buy newspapers. Special constables were sworn in by the hundred. Later on, when it became known that the insurgent forces were really on their southward march, a proclamation was issued, ordering a general day of humiliation, with services in all the churches, and prayers for the safety of Religion and the Realm. The Archbishop of Canterbury herself performed the service at Westminster Abbey, and the Bishop of London at St Paul's.

Meantime, spite of law and orders, the country-people flocked from all sides to see the gallant show of Lord Chester's little army. Captain Dunquerque led the van, which consisted of fifty stalwart keepers. At the head of the main body rode the Chief, clad in scarlet, with glittering helmet; with him were the officers of his Staff, also gallantly dressed and splendidly mounted. Next came, marching in fours, his army of three hundred sturdy countrymen, armed with rifle and bayonet; after them marched the younger men, some mere lads, carrying guns of all descriptions, pikes, and even sticks,—not one among these that did not carry a cockade: their banner, borne by two of the strongest, was of red silk, with the words, 'We will be free!' An immense crowd of women looked on as they started: some of them cursed and screamed; but the girls laughed. Then other men of the villages broke away from their wives and sisters, and marched beside the soldiers, trying to keep in step, snatching their cockades, and shouting with them. Last of all came a little band of twenty-five, mounted, who served to keep the crowd from pressing too closely, and guarded a carriage and four, in which were the Bishop, the Professor, and the two girls. They sat up to their knees in scarlet cockades and rosettes, which the girls were making up and the Professor was distributing.

In this order they marched. After the first few hours, it was found that, besides a great number of recruits, the army had been joined by at least a hundred village girls, who walked with them and refused to go back. They followed their sweethearts. 'Let us keep them,' said the Professor: 'they will be useful to us.'

At the next halting-place she had all these girls drawn up before her, and made them a speech. She told them that if they desired a hand in the great work, they might do their part: they would be allowed to join the army on condition of marching apart from the men; of not interfering with them in any way; of doing what they were told to do, and of carrying a banner. To this they readily consented, being, in fact, to one woman, enraged with the existing order of things, and caring very little about being the mistress if they could not have their own lovers. And in the end, they proved most valuable and useful allies.

Whenever they passed a house, Lord Chester sent half a dozen men to seize upon whatever arms they could find, and all the ammunition, if there was any. They had orders, also, to bring out the men, whom the officers inspected; and if there were any young fellow among them, they offered him a place in their ranks. A good many guns were got in this way, but very few men,—the young men of the middle class being singularly spiritless. They had not the healthy outdoor life, with riding, shooting, and athletics, that men of Lord Chester's rank enjoyed; nor had they the outdoor work and companionship which hardened the nerves of the farm-labourers. Mostly, therefore, they gazed with wonder and terror at the spectacle; and on being brought out and harangued, meekly replied that they would rather stay at home, and retired amid the jeers of the soldiers.

Several pleasant surprises were experienced. At one house, the squire, a jolly fox-hunting old fellow, turned out with his four sons, all well mounted, and brought with him a dozen good rifles with a large supply of ammunition. The old fellow remarked that he was sixty-five years of age, and had been wishing all his life, and so had his father and his grandfather before him, to put an end to the intolerable upside-down condition of things. 'And mind, my lady,' he shouted to his wife and daughters, who were standing by, filled with rage and consternation, 'you and the girls, when we get back again, will sing another tune, or I will know the reason why!' Nor was this the only instance.

When they marched through a village the trumpets blew, the drums beat, the soldiers shouted and sang; then the men were brought out, and invited to join; the place was searched for arms, and the company of women ran about congratulating the girls of the place on the approaching abolition of Forced Marriages.

The first day's march covered twenty miles. The army had passed through five villages and one small town; they had seized on about two hundred guns of all kinds, and a considerable quantity of ammunition; they had increased their ranks by two hundred and fifty strong and lusty fellows. The evening was not allowed to be wasted in singing and shouting. Drill was renewed, and the new-comers taught the first elements of marching in step and line. For the first time, too, they attempted a sham fight, with sad blunders, as may be imagined.

'They are good material,' said the Professor, 'but your army has yet to be formed.'

'If only,' murmured Clarence, 'they would listen to my preaching.'

'They have had too much preaching all their lives,' said the Bishop. 'We will conquer first, and preach afterwards. Let us pray that there may be no bloodshed.'

The second day's march was like the first; but the little army was now swelling beyond all expectations. At the close of the second day it numbered a thousand, and commissariat difficulties began. Here the company of women proved useful. They were all country girls, able to ride and drive; they 'borrowed' the carts of the farm-houses, and, escorted by soldiers, drove about the country requisitioning provisions. It became necessary to have wagons: these also were borrowed, and in a short time the army dragged at its heels an immense train of wagons loaded with ammunition, provisions, and stores of all kinds. For everything that was taken, an order for its value was left behind, stamped with the signature of 'Chester.'

At the close of the second day's march, being then near Bury St Edmunds, they were two thousand strong; at the end of the third, being on Newmarket Heath, they were five thousand; and here, because the place was open and the position good, a halt of three days was resolved upon, in which the men might be drilled, taught to act together, and divided into corps; also, sham fights would be fought, and the men, some of whom were little more than boys, could grow accustomed to the discharge of guns and the use of their weapons. The camp was protected by sentinels, and the cavalry scoured the country for recruits and information. As yet no sign had been made by the Government. But on Sunday morning, being the third day of the halt, the scouts brought in a deputation from the House of Peeresses, consisting of two Sisters of the Holy Preaching Order, and a guard of twenty-five policewomen. Lord Chester and his staff rode out to meet them.

'What is your message?' he asked.

'The terms offered by the House to the insurgents,' replied one of the Sisters, 'are, first laying down of arms, and dispersion of the men; secondly, the immediate submission of the leaders.'

'And what then?' asked Lord Chester.

'Justice,' replied the Sister sternly. 'Now stand aside and let us address the men.'

Lord Chester laughed.

'Go call a dozen of the women's company,' he ordered. 'Now,' when they came, 'take these two Sisters, and march them through the camp with drum and fife. These are the women who are trained to terrify the men with lying threats, false fears, and vain superstitions. As for you policewomen, you can go back and tell the House that I will myself inform them of my terms.'

The officers of law looked at each other. They saw before them spread out the white tents of the camp, the splendid army, the glittering weapons, the brilliant uniforms, the flags, the noise and tumult of the camp, and they were afraid. Presently they beheld, with consternation, the most singular procession ever formed. First went the drums and fifes; then came, handcuffed, the two Holy Preaching Sisters—they were clad in their sacred white robes, to touch which was sacrilege; behind them ran and danced the troop of village girls, shouting, pointing, singing their new songs about Love and Freedom; and the soldiers came forth from their tents clapping their hands and applauding. But the Bishop sent word that they were to be stripped of their white robes and turned out of the camp. It was in ragged flannel petticoats that the poor Sisters regained their friends, and in woeful plight of mind as well as of body.

The three days' halt finished, Lord Chester gave the word to advance. And now his army, he thought, was large enough to meet any number of Convict Wardens who might be sent against him. He had eight thousand men, hastily drilled, but full of ardour; he had a picked corps of five hundred guards, consisting of his faithful gamekeepers and the men who had been always with gentlemen about their sports. These were good shots, and pretty sure to be steady even under fire. He had five hundred cavalry, mostly mounted well, and consisting of farmers' sons, officered by the fox-hunting squire, his four sons, and a few other gentlemen who had come in. The difficulty now was to admit all who crowded to the camp. For the news had spread over all England, and the roads were crowded with young fellows flying from their homes, defying the rural police, to join Lord Chester's camp.

The time was come for a bold stroke. It was resolved to leave Jack Kennion—greatly to his discontent, but there was no help—behind, to receive recruits, and form an army of reserve. Lord Chester himself, with the main body and Algy Dunquerque, was to press on. The boldest stroke of all was the surprise of London, and this it was decided to attempt. For by this time the ardour of the troops was beyond the most sanguine hopes of the leaders: the submissiveness of three generations had disappeared in a week; the meek and docile lads whose wives received the pay, and ordered them to go and sit at home when there was no work to do, were changed into hardy, reckless, and enthusiastic soldiers. Turenne himself had not a more daredevil lot. They were nearly all young; they had never before been free for a single day; they rejoiced in their new

companionship; they gloried in the sham fights, the wrestling, the single-stick—all the games with which the fighting spirit was awakened in them. As for the march, it was splendid: they sang as they went; if they did not sing, they laughed—the joy of laughter was previously unknown to these lads. The ruling sex did not laugh among themselves, nor did they understand the masculine yearning for mirth. In the upper classes jesting was ill-bred, and in the lower it was irreligious. Irreligious! Why, in this short time the whole army had thrown off their religion.
All over the country the men were rising and rushing to join Lord Chester. The great conspiracy was not alone answerable for this sudden impulse; nor, indeed, had the conspirators been successful in the towns, where the spirit of the men had been effectually crushed by long isolation. Here, however, the leaflets distributed among the girls bore good fruit. Not a household in the country but was now fiercely divided between those who welcomed the rebellion and those who hated and dreaded the success of the men: on the one side, orthodoxy, age, conservatism; on the other, youth, and the dream of an easy life, rendered easier by the work and devotion of a lover. So that, though the towns remained outwardly quiet, they were ready for the occupation of the rebels.
The army presented now an appearance very different from the ragged regiment which sallied forth from the gates of the Park. They were dressed in uniform: the guards wore a dark-green tunic—only proved shots were admitted into their body; the cavalry were in scarlet, the line were in scarlet; the artillery wore dark-green. All the men were armed with rifles. Of course, the uniforms were not in all cases complete, yet every day improved them; for among the volunteers were tailors, cobblers, and handicraftsmen of all kinds, whose services were given in their own trades. The great banner, with the words 'We will be free!' was carried after the Chief, and in the rear marched the company of a hundred girls, also in a kind of uniform, carrying their banner, 'Give us back our sweethearts!'
The line of march was kept as much as possible away from the towns, because it was thought advisable not to irritate the municipalities until the time came when they could be gently upset; also, the material of the men in the towns was not of the sturdy kind with which they hoped to win their battles.
Nothing more was heard of the House of Peeresses. What, then, were they doing? They were holding meetings in the morning, and wrangling. No one knew what to propose. They had sent executive officers of the law to the camp; these had been contemptuously told to go back. They had summoned the leaders to lay down their arms; they had been informed that Lord Chester would dictate his own terms. They had sent Preaching Sisters,—the most eloquent, the most persuasive, the most sacred: they had been stripped of their sacred robes, tied to a cart-tail, and driven through the camp by women, amid the derision of women—actually women! What more could they do?
The army was reported as marching southwards by rapid marches, headed by Lord Chester. They passed Bury St Edmunds and Cambridge, without, however, entering the town. They recruited as they went; so that beside the regularly drilled men, now veterans of a fortnight or so, it was reported that the line of march was followed for miles by runaway boys, apprentices, grooms, artisans, and labourers shouting for Lord Chester and for liberty. All these things, and worse, were hourly reported to the distracted House.
'And what are we doing?' shrieked the Duchess of Dunstanburgh. 'What are we doing but talk? Are we, then, fallen so low, that at the first movement of an enemy we have nothing but tears and recrimination? Is this a time to accuse me—ME—of forcing the rebel chief into rebellion? Is it not a time to act? When the rebellion is subdued, when the Chief is hanged, and his miserable

followers flogged—yes, flogged at the very altars they have derided—let us resume the strife of tongues. In the name of our sex, in the name of our religion, let us Act.'

They looked at each other, but no one proposed the only step left to them. Lady Carlyon was no longer among them. She would attend no more sittings. The clamour of tongues humiliated her. She sat alone in her house in Park Lane, thinking sadly of what might happen.

'On me,' said the Duchess solemnly, 'devolves the duty, the painful duty, of reminding the House that there is but one way to meet rebellion. All human institutions, even when, like our own, they are of Divine origin, are based upon—Force. Law is an idle sound without—Force. Duty, religion, obedience, rest ultimately upon—Force. These men have dared to band themselves together against law, order, and religion. We must remember that they represent a very small, a really insignificant, section of the men of this country. It is cheering, at this moment of gloom and distress, to receive by every post letters from every municipality in the country expressing the loyalty of the towns. Order reigns everywhere, except where this turbulent boy is leading his troops—to destruction. I use this word with the utmost reluctance; but I must use this word. I say—destruction. Among the ranks of that army are men known to many in this House. My own gamekeepers, many of my own tenants' sons and husbands, are in that rabble-rout of raw, undisciplined, and imperfectly armed rustics. Yet I say—destruction. We have now but one thing to do. Call out our prison-guards, and let loose these fierce and angry hounds upon the foe. I wait for the approval of the House.'

All lifted their hands, but in silence; for they were sadly conscious that they were sending the gallant, if mistaken fellows to death, and bringing sorrow upon innocent homes. The House separated, and for a while there was no more recrimination. The Duchess called a Cabinet Council, and that night messengers sped in all directions to bring together the Convict Guards— not only the two thousand first ordered to be in readiness, but as many as could be spared. It was resolved to replace them by men chosen from the prisoners, whose cases, in return for their service, should have favourable consideration. By forced marches, and by seizing on every possible means of conveyance, it was reckoned that they could muster some ten thousand,—all strong, desperate villains, capable of anything, and a match for twice that number of raw village lads.

They came up in driblets—here a hundred and there a hundred—from the various prisons throughout the country: they were men of rough and coarse appearance; they wore an ugly yellow uniform; they bore themselves as if they were ashamed of their calling, which certainly was the most repulsive of any; they showed neither ardour for the work before them nor any kind of fear.

They were received by clerks of the Prison Department, who sent them off to camp in Hyde Park, where rations of some kind were prepared for them. The clerks showed them scant courtesy, which, indeed, they seemed to take as a matter of course; and once established in their camp, they gave no trouble, keeping quite to themselves, and patiently waiting orders.

Three days were thus expended. The excitement of the town was frightful. Business was suspended, prayers were offered at all the churches every morning, the men were most carefully kept from associating together, constables patrolled in parties of four all night long, and continually the post-girls came galloping along the roads bringing the news. 'They are coming, they are coming!' Oh, what was the Government about? Could they do nothing, then? What was the use of the Convict Wardens, unless they were to be sent out to arrest the leaders, and shoot all who refused to disband and disperse? But there were not wanting ominous whispers among the crowds of wild talkers. What, it was asked, would happen if the men did come? They would take the power into their own hands. Very good. It could not be in worse hands than Lady Dunstanburgh's. They would turn the women out of the Professions. Very well, said the younger women. They only starved in the Professions; and if the men were in power, they would have to find homes and food at least for their sisters and wives. Let them come.

In three days Lord Chester was at Bishop-Stortford. Next, he was reported to be encamped in Epping Forest. His cavalry had seized the arsenal at Enfield, which, with carelessness incredible, had been left in charge of two aged women. This gave him a dozen pieces of ordnance. He was on the march from Epping; he was but a few miles from London; contradictory rumours and reports of all kinds flew wildly about; he was going to massacre, pillage, and plunder everything; he was afraid to advance farther; he would destroy all the churches; he was restrained at the last moment by respect for the faith in which he had been brought up; his men had mutinied; his men clamoured to be led on London. All these reports, and more, were whispered from one to the other. What was quite certain was, that the Convict Wardens were all arrived, and were under orders to march early in the morning. And it was also certain, because girls who had ventured on the north roads had seen them, that the rebels were encamped on Hampstead Heath, and it was said that they were in high spirits—singing, dancing, and drinking. No one knew how many they were—thousands upon thousands, and all armed.

There was little sleep in London during that night. The married women remained at home to calm the excitement of the men, now getting beyond their control. The unmarried women flocked by thousands to Hyde Park to look at the tents of the Convict Wardens, now called the Army of Avengers. In every tent eight men, more than a thousand tents; ten thousand men; the fiercest, bravest, most experienced of men. What a lesson, what a terrible lesson, would the rebels learn next morning!

CHAPTER XIII. THE NIGHT BEFORE THE BATTLE

IT was evening when the rebel leader stood upon the heights of Hampstead and looked before him, by the light of the setting sun, upon the hazy and indistinct mass of the great city which he was come to conquer. Behind him his ten thousand men, with twice ten thousand followers, were erecting their tents and setting up the camp with a mighty bustle, noise, and clamour. Yet there was no confusion. Thanks to the administrative capacity of Algy Dunquerque, all was done in order. The Professor, who had left her carriage, stood beside Lord Chester. He was dismounted, and, with the aid of a glass, was trying to make out familiar towers in the golden mist that rested upon the great city.

'So far, my lord, we have sped well,' she said softly.

He started at her voice.

'Well, indeed, my dear Professor,' he replied. 'I would to-morrow were over.'

'Fear not; your men will answer to your call.'

'I do not fear. They are brave fellows. Yet—to think that their blood must be spilt!'

'There spoke Lord Chester of the past, not the gallant Prince of the present. Why, what if a few hundreds of dead men strew this field to-morrow provided the Right prevails? Of what good is a man's life to him, if he does not give it for the sacred cause? To give a life—why, it is to lend a thing; to hasten the slow course of time; to make the soul take at a single leap the immortality which comes to others so slowly. Fear not for the blood of martyrs, my lord.'

'You always cheer and comfort me, Professor.'

'It is because I am a woman,' she replied. 'Let me fulfil the highest function of my sex.'

They were interrupted by an aide-de-camp, who came galloping across the Heath.

'From Captain Dunquerque, my lord,' he began. 'The Convict Wardens are encamped in force in Hyde Park; they number ten thousand, and have got thirty guns; they march to-morrow morning.'

'Very good,' said the Chief; and the young officer fell back.

'Ten thousand strong!' said the Professor. 'Then they have left the prisons almost without a guard. When these are dispersed, where will they find a new army? They are delivered into your hands.'

Hampstead Heath may be approached by two or three roads: there is the direct road up Haverstock Hill; or there is the way by the Gospel Oak and the Vale of Health; or, again, there is the road from the north, or that from Highgate. But the way by which the Convict Wardens would march from Hyde Park was most certainly that of Haverstock Hill; and they would emerge upon the Heath by one of the narrow roads known as Holly Hill, Heath Street, and the Grove,—probably by all three. Or they might attempt the upper part of the Heath by the Vale of Health.

The plan of battle was agreed to with very little debate, because it was simple.

The cannon, loaded with grape-shot and masked by bushes, were drawn up to command these three streets.

Behind the cannon the Guards were to lie, ready to spring to their feet and send in a volley after the first discharge of grape-shot.

The cavalry were to be posted among the trees, on the spot called after a once famous tavern which formerly stood there—Jack Straw's Castle; the infantry, now divided into five battalions, each two thousand strong, were to lie in their places behind the Guards. These simple arrangements made, the Chief rode into the camp to encourage the men.

They needed little encouragement; the men were in excellent spirits; the news that they would have to fight those enemies of mankind, the Convict Wardens, filled them with joy. Not one among them all but had some friend, some relation, immured within the gloomy prisons, for disobedience, mutiny, or violence; some had themselves experienced the rigours of imprisonment, and the tender mercies of the ruffians who were allowed to maintain discipline with rod and lash, rifle and bayonet. These were the men who were coming out to shoot them down! Very good; they should see.

Lord Chester and his Staff rode about the camp, making speeches, cheering the men, drinking with them, and encouraging them. Their liberties, he told them, were in their own hand: one victory, and the cause was won. Then he inspired them with contempt as well as hatred for their opponents. They were men who could shoot down a flying prisoner, but had never stood face to face with a foe: they were coming out, expecting to find a meek herd, who would fly at the first shot; in their place they would meet an army of Englishmen. The men shouted and cheered: their spirit was up. And later on, about ten o'clock, a strange thing happened. No one ever knew how it began, or who set it going; but from man to man the word was passed. Then all the army rose to their feet, and shouted for joy; then the company of girls came, and shed tears among them, but for joy; and some, including the girl they had called Susan, fell upon the necks of their old sweethearts, and kissed them, bidding them be brave, and fight like men; and those who were old men wept, because this good thing had come too late for them.

For the word was—Divorce!

The young men, they said, were to abandon the wives they had been forced to marry. With Victory they were to win Love!

It was about ten o'clock when Lord Chester sought the Bishop's tent. He had just concluded an

Evening Service, and was sitting with his wife, his daughters, and Clarence Veysey. With the Chief came Algernon Dunquerque.

'We are here,' said Lord Chester, 'for a few words—it may be of farewell. My Lord Bishop, are you contented with your pupils?'

'I give you all,' he said solemnly, 'my blessing. Go on and prosper. But as we may fail and so die, because victory is not of man, let those who have aught to say to each other say it now.'

Algernon spoke first, though all looked at each other.

'I love your daughter Faith. Give us your consent, my Lord Bishop, before we go out to fight.'

The Bishop took the girl by the hand, and gave her to the young man, saying, 'Blessed be thou, O my daughter!'

Then Clarence Veysey spoke likewise, and asked for Grace; and with such words did the father give her to him.

'Now,' said Algernon, 'there needs no more. If we fall, we fall together.'

'Yes,' said Grace quietly, 'we should not survive the cause.'

'I hope,' said Lord Chester, smiling gravely, 'that one of you will live at least long enough to take my last message to Lady Carlyon. You will tell her, Grace, or you, my dear Professor, that my last thought was for her.' But as he spoke the curtain of the tent was pulled aside, and Constance herself stood before them.

She was pale, and tears were in her eyes. She wore a riding-habit; but it was covered with dust.

'Edward!' she cried. 'Fly ... fly ... while there is time! All of you fly!'

'What is it, Constance? How came you here?'

'I came because I can bear it no longer. I came to warn you, and to help your escape, if that may be. The Duchess has issued a warrant for my arrest,—for High Treason: that is nothing,' with a proud gesture. 'They will say I ran away from the warrant: that is false. Edward, your life is gone unless you are twenty miles from London to-morrow!'

'Come, Constance,' said the Professor, 'you are hot and tired. Rest a little; drink some water; take breath. We are prepared, I think, for all that you can tell us.'

'Oh, no!... no!... you cannot be. Listen! They have ten thousand Convict Wardens in Hyde Park ...'

'We know this,' said Algernon.

'Who will attack you to-morrow.'

'We know this too.'

'Their orders are to shoot down all without parley; all—do you hear?—who are found with arms. The Chiefs are to be taken to the Tower!' she shuddered.

'We know all this, Constance,' said Lord Chester.

'You know it! and you can look unconcerned?'

'Not unconcerned entirely, but resigned perhaps, and even hopeful.'

'Edward, what can you do?'

'If they have orders to shoot all who do not fly, my men, for their part, have orders not to fly, but to shoot all who stand in their way.'

'Your men? Poor farm-labourers! what can they do?'

'Wait till morning, Constance, and you shall see. Is there anything else you can tell me?'

'Yes. After the Wardens have dispersed the rebels, the Horse Guards are to be ordered out to ride them down.'

'Oh!' said Lord Chester. 'Well ... after we are dispersed, we will consider the question of the riding down. Then we need not expect the Horse Guards to-morrow morning?'

'No; they will come afterwards.'

'Thank you, Constance; you have given me one piece of intelligence. I confess I was uncertain about the Guards. And now, dear child,'—he called her, the late Home Secretary, 'dear child,'—'as this is a solemn night, and we have much to think of and to do ... one word before we part. Constance, you have by this act of yours, cast in your lot with us, because you thought to save my life. Everything is risked upon to-morrow's victory. If we fail we die. Are you ready to die with me?'

She made no reply. The old feeling, the overwhelming force of the man, made her cheek white and her heart faint. She held out her hands.

He took her—before all those witnesses—in his arms, and kissed her on the forehead. 'Stay with us, my darling,' he whispered; 'cast in your lot with mine.'

She had no power to resist, none to refuse. She was conquered; Man was stronger than Woman.

'Children,' said the Bishop solemnly, 'you shall not die, but live.'

Constance started. She knew not this kind of language, which was borrowed from the Books of the Ancient Faith.

'There are many things,' said the Bishop, 'of which you know not yet, Lady Carlyon. After to-morrow we will instruct you. Meantime it is late; the Chief has business; I would be alone. Go you with my daughters and rest, if you can, until the morning.'

The very atmosphere seemed strange to Constance: the young men in authority, the women submissive; this old man speaking as if he were a learned divine, reverend, grave, and accustomed to be heard; and, outside, the voices of men ringing, of arms clashing, of music playing,—all the noise of a camp before it settles into rest for the night.

'Can they,' Constance whispered to Grace Ingleby, looking round her outside the tent—'will they dare to fight these terrible and cruel Convict Wardens?'

'Oh, Lady Carlyon!' Grace replied, 'you do not know, you cannot guess, what wonderful things Lord Chester has done with the men in the last fortnight. From poor, obedient slaves, he has made them men indeed.'

'Men!' Constance saw that she could not understand the word in the sense to which she had been accustomed.

'Surely you know,' Grace went on, 'that our object is more than we have ventured to proclaim. We began with the cry of "Youth for the Young." That touched a grievance which was more felt, perhaps, in country districts, where men retained some of their independence, than in towns. But we meant very much more. We shall abolish the Established Church, and the supremacy of Woman. Man will reign once more, and will worship, after the manner of his ancestors, the real living Divine Man, instead of the shadowy Perfect Woman.'

'Oh!' Constance heard and trembled. 'And we—what shall we do?'

'We shall take our own place—we shall be the housewives; we shall be loving and faithful servants to men, and they will be our servants in return. Love knows no mastery. Yet man must rule outside the house.'

'Oh!' Constance could say no more.

'Believe me, this is the true place of woman; she is the giver of happiness and love; she is the mother and the wife. As for us, we have reigned and have tried to rule. How much we have failed, no one knows better than yourself.'

Grace guided her companion to a great marquee, where the company of girls, sobered now, and rather tearful, because their sweethearts were to go a-fighting in earnest on the morrow, were making lint and bandages.

'I must go on with my work,' said Grace. Her sister Faith was already in her place, tearing, cutting and shaping. 'Do you lie down' here is a pile of lint—make that your bed, and sleep if you can.'

Constance lay down; but she could not sleep. She already heard in imagination the tramp of the cruel Convict Wardens; she saw her lover and his companions shot down; she was herself a prisoner; then, with a cry, she sprang to her feet.

'Give me some work to do,' she said to Grace; 'I cannot sleep.'

They made a place for her, Grace and Faith between them, saying nothing.

By this time the girls were all silent, and some were crying; for the day was dawning—the day when these terrible preparations of lint would be used for poor wounded men.

When, about half-past five, the first rays of the September sun poured into the marquee upon the group of women, Grace sprang to her feet, crying aloud in a kind of ecstacy.

'The day has come—the day is here! Oh, what can we do but pray!'

She threw herself upon her knees and prayed aloud, while all wept and sobbed.

Constance knelt with the rest, but the prayer touched her not. She was only sad, while Grace sorrowed with faith and hope.

Then Faith Ingleby raised her sweet strong voice, and, with her, the girls sang together a hymn which was unknown to Constance. It began:—

Awake, my soul, and with the sun
Thy daily course of duty run.

This act of worship and submission done, they returned to their work. Outside, the camp began gradually to awaken. Before six o'clock the fires were lit, and the men's breakfast was getting ready; by seven o'clock everything was done—tents struck, arms piled, men accoutred.

Constance went out to look at the strange sight of the rebel army. Her heart beat when she looked upon the novel scene.

Regiments were forming, companies marching into place, flags flying, drums beating, and trumpets calling. And the soldiers!—saw one ever such men before? They were marching, heads erect and flashing eyes; the look of submission gone—for ever. Yes; these men might be shot down, but they could never be reduced to their old condition.

'There is the Chief,' said Faith Ingleby.

He stood without his tent, his Staff about him, looking round him. Authority was on his brow; he was indeed, Constance felt with sinking heart, that hitherto incredible thing—a Man in command.

'We girls have no business here,' said Faith; 'let us go back to our tent.'

But as she spoke, Lord Chester saw them; and leaving his Staff, he walked across the Heath, bearing his sword in his hand, followed by Algernon Dunquerque.

'Constance,' he said gravely, 'buckle my sword for me before the battle.'

She did it, trembling and tearful. Then, while Faith Ingleby did the same office for Algernon, he took her in his arms and kissed her lips in the sight of all the army. Every man took it as a lesson for himself. He was to fight for love as well as liberty. A deafening shout rent the air.

Then Lord Chester sprang upon his horse and rode to the front.

Everything was now in readiness. The cannon, masked by bushes, were protected by the pond in front; on either side were the guards ready to lie down; behind them, the regiments, massed at present, but prepared for open order; and in the trees could be seen the gleaming helmets and swords of the cavalry.

'Let us go to my father,' said Faith; 'he and Clarence will pray for us.'

'Algy,' said Lord Chester cheerfully, 'what are you thinking of?'
'I was thinking how sorry Jack Kennion will be to have missed this day.'

And then there happened the most remarkable, the most surprising thing in the whole of this surprising campaign. There was a movement among the men in front, followed by loud laughing and shouting; and then a party of girls, some of the Company of women which followed the army, came flying across the Heath breathless, because they had run all the way from Marble Arch to convey their news.

'They have run away, my lord!' they cried all together.

'Who have run away?'

'The Army of Avengers—the Convict Wardens. They have all run away, and there is not one left.'

'Run away? What does it mean? Why did they run away?'

Then the girls looked at each other and laughed, but were a little ashamed, because they were not quite sure how the Chief would take it.

'It seemed such a pity,' said one of them, presently, 'that any of our own brave fellows should be killed.'

'Such a dreadful pity,' they murmured.

'And by such cruel men.'

'Such cruel, horrible men,' they echoed.

'So that we ... we stole into the camp when they were asleep and we frightened them; and they all ran away, leaving their arms behind them.'

Lord Chester looked at Captain Dunquerque.

'Woman's wit,' he said. 'Would you and I have thought of such a trick? Go, girls, tell the Bishop.'

But Algy looked sad.

'And after all this drilling,' he said, with a sigh, 'and all our shouting, there is to be no fighting!'

CHAPTER XIV. THE ARMY OF AVENGERS

THE awful nature of the crisis, and the strangeness of the sight, kept the streets in the neighbourhood of the Camp in Hyde Park full of women, young and old. They roamed about among the tents, looking at the sullen faces of the men, examining their arms, and gazing upon them curiously, as if they were wild beasts. Not one among them expressed the least friendliness or kind feeling. The men were regarded by those who paid them, as well as by the rebels, with undisguised loathing.

About midnight the crowd lessened; at two o'clock, though there were still a few stragglers, most of the curious and anxious politicians had gone home to bed; at three, some of them still remained; at four—the darkest and deadest time of an autumn night—all were gone home, every special constable even, and the Camp was left in silence, the men in their tents, and asleep.

There still remained, however, a little crowd of some two or three dozen girls; they were collected together about the Marble Arch. They had formed, during the evening, part of the crowd; but now that this was dispersed, they seemed to gather together, and to talk in whispers. Presently, as if some resolution was arrived at, they all poured into the Park, and entered the sleeping Camp.

The men were lying down, mostly asleep; but they were not undressed, so as to be ready for their early march. No sentries were on duty, nor was there any watch kept.

Presently the girls found, in the darkness, a cart containing drums. They seized them and began drumming with all their might. Then they separated, and ran about from tent to tent; they pulled and haled the sleepers, startled by the drums, into terrified wakefulness; they cried as soon as their men were wide awake, 'Wake up all!—wake up!—run for your lives!—the rebels will be on us in ten minutes! They are a hundred thousand strong: run for your lives!—they have sworn to hang every Convict Warden who is not shot. Oh, run, run, run!' Then they ran to the next tent, and similarly exhorted its sleepers. Consider the effect of this nocturnal alarm. The men slept eight in a tent. There were about thirty girls, and somewhat more than a thousand tents. It is creditable to the girls that the thirty made so much noise that they seemed like three thousand to the startled soldiers. To be awakened suddenly in the dead of night, to be told that their enemies were upon them, to hear cries and screams of warning, with the beating of drums, produced exactly the consequences that were expected. The men, who had no experience of collective action, who had no officers, who had no heart for their work, were bewildered; they ran about here and there, asking where was the enemy: then shots were heard, for the girls found the rifles and fired random shots in the air; and then a panic followed, and they fled—fled in wild terror, running in every direction, leaving their guns behind them in the tents, so that in a quarter of an hour there was not one single man of all the Army of Avengers left in the Camp.

The orders were that the march should begin about six o'clock in the morning—that is, as soon after sunrise as was possible.

It was also ordered that the Army of Avengers should be followed by the Head of the Police Department, Lady Princetown, with her assistant secretaries, clerks, and officers, and that they should be supplied with tumbrils for the conveyance to prison of any who might escape the vengeance prepared for them and be taken prisoners.

At a quarter past six o'clock an orderly clerk proceeded to the Camp. To her great joy the Camp was empty; she did not observe the guns lying about, but as there were no men visible, she concluded that the Army was already on the march. She returned and reported the fact.

Then the order of the Police Procession was rapidly arranged; and it too followed, as they thought, the march of the Avengers.

By this time a good many women were in the streets or at the windows of the houses. Most of the streets were draped with black hangings, in token of general shame and woe that man should be found so inexpressibly guilty. The church bells tolled a knell; a service of humiliation was going on in all of them, but men were not allowed to participate. It was felt that it was safer for them to be at home. Consequently, the strange spectacle of a whole city awake and ready for the day's work, without a single man visible, was, for one morning only, seen in London.

The Police Procession formed in Whitehall, and slowly moved north. It was headed by Lady Princetown, riding, with her two assistant secretaries; after them came the chief clerks and senior clerks of the Department, followed by the messengers, police constables, and servants, who walked; after them followed, with a horrible grumbling and grinding of wheels, the six great black tumbrils intended for the prisoners.

The march was through Regent Street, Oxford Street, the Tottenham Court Road, Chalk Farm, and so up Haverstock Hill. Everywhere the streets were lined with women, who looked after the dreadful signs of punishment with pity and terror, even though they acknowledged the justice and necessity of the step.

These men, they told each other, had torn down Religion, scoffed at things holy, and proclaimed divorce where the husband had been forced to marry; they pretended that theirs was the right to rule; they were going to destroy every social institution. Should such wretches be allowed to live?

Yet, always, the whisper, the suspicion, the doubt, the question, put not in words, but by looks and gestures,—'What have we women done that we should deserve to rule? and which among us does not know that the Religion of the Perfect Woman was only invented by ourselves for the better suppression of man? Who believes it? What have we done with Love?'

And the sight, the actual sight, of those officers of law going forth to bring in the prisoners, was a dreadful thing to witness.

Meantime, what were the Army of Avengers doing?

Slaughtering, shooting down, bayoneting, no doubt. No farther off than the heights of Hampstead their terrible work was going on. It spoke well for the zeal of these devoted soldiers that they had marched so early in the morning that no one had seen them go by. Very odd, that no one at all had seen them. Would Lord Chester escape? And what—oh what!—would be done with Lady Carlyon, Professor Ingleby and her two daughters, and the crowd of girls who had flocked to London with the rebels? Hanging—mere hanging—was far too good for them. Let them be tortured.

The Procession reached the top of Haverstock Hill. Hampstead Hill alone remained. In a short time the relentless Lady Princetown would be on the field of action. Strange, not only that no sign of the Army had been seen, but that no firing had been heard! Could Lord Chester have fled with all his men?

Now just before the Police Procession reached the Heath, they were astonished by a clattering of mounted soldiers, richly dressed and gallantly armed, who rode down the narrow streets of the town and surrounded them. They were a detachment of cavalry headed by Captain Dunquerque, who saluted Lady Princetown laughing. All the men laughed too.

'I have the honour,' he said, 'to invite your ladyship to take a seat in a tumbril. You are my prisoner.'

'Where—where—where is the Army?'

'You mean the Convict Wardens? They fled before daylight. Come, my lads, time presses.'

They were actually in the hands of the enemy!

In a few moments the whole of the Chiefs of the great Police Department were being driven in the rumbling black tumbrils, followed by the Lancers, towards the rebel camp. They looked at each other in sheer despair.

'As for you women,' said Captain Dunquerque, addressing the clerks and constables, 'you can go free. Disperse! Vanish!'

He left them staring at each other. Presently a few turned and hurried down the Hill to spread the news. But the greater part followed timidly, but spurred by curiosity, into the Camp.

Here, what marvels met their eyes!

Men, such as they had never dreamed of, bravely dressed, and bearing themselves with a gallant masterfulness which frightened those who saw it for the first time. Presently a trumpet blew and the men fell in. Then the astonished women saw that wonderful thing, the evolutions of an army. The regiments were drawn up in a great hollow square. At one corner stood the fatal black tumbril with Lady Princetown and her aides sitting dolefully and in amazement. Bands of music stood in the centre. Presently Lord Chester, the Chief, rode in with his Staff, and the bands broke out in triumphal strains.

'Men of England!' he cried, 'our enemies have fled. There is no longer any opposition. We march on London immediately.'

The shouts of the soldiers rent the air. When silence was possible, the Bishop, venerable in lawn-sleeves and cassock, spoke,—
'I proclaim Edward, sometime called Earl of Chester, lawful hereditary King of Great Britain and Ireland. God save the King!'
Then the officers of the Staff did homage, bending the knee and kissing the hand of their Sovereign. And the bands struck up again, playing the old and wellnigh forgotten air 'God save the King!' And the soldiers shouted again. And Lady Princetown saw, indeed, that the supremacy of women was gone.

Then the march on London was resumed.
After the advance-cavalry came the Guards, preceding and following the King. Before him was borne the Royal Standard, made long ago for such an occasion by Grace and Faith Ingleby. The bands played and the soldiers sang 'God save the King' along the streets. The houses were crowded with women's faces—some anxious, some sad, some angry, some rejoicing, but all frightened; and the wrath of those who were wrathful waxed fiercer when the company of girls followed the soldiers, dressed in 'loyal' ribbons and such finery as they could command, and singing, like the men, 'God save the King.'

The House of Peeresses was sitting in permanence. Some of the ladies had been sitting all night; a few had fallen asleep; a few more had come to the House early, unable to keep away. They all looked anxious and haggard.
At nine o'clock the first of the fugitives from the Police Procession arrived, and brought the dreadful news that the Army of Avengers had dispersed without striking a blow, that Lady Princetown was a prisoner, and that the rebels would probably march on London without delay. Then the Duchess of Dunstanburgh informed the terror-stricken House that she had ordered out the three regiments of Guards. They were to be hurled, she said, at the rebels; they would serve to harass and keep them in check while a new army was gathered together. She exhorted the Peeresses to remain calm and collected, and, above all, to be assured that there was not the slightest reason for alarm.
Alas! the barracks were empty!
What then, had become of the Guards?
At the first news of the dispersion of the Avengers, the wives of the Guardsmen, acting with one common consent, made for the barracks and dragged away the soldiers, every woman her own husband to her own home, where she defied the clerks of the War Office, who rushed about trying to get the men together. For greater safety the women hid away the boots—those splendid boots without which the Horse Guards would be but as common men. Of the three thousand, there remained only two orphan drummer-boys and a sergeant, a widower without sisters. To hurl this remnant against Lord Chester was manifestly too absurd even for the clerks of the War Office. Besides, they refused to go.
On the top of this dreadful news, the House was informed by the Chancellor that the officers sent to carry out the arrest of Lady Carlyon reported that her ladyship had fled, and was now in Lord Chester's camp with the rebels.
What next?
'The next thing, ladies,' said a middle-aged Peeress who had been conspicuous all her life for nothing in the world except an entire want of interest in political questions, 'is that our reign is over. Man has taken the power in his own hands. For my own part, I am only astonished that he

has waited so long. It needed nothing but the courage of one young fellow to light the fire with a single spark. I propose that a vote of thanks be passed to her Grace the Duchess of Dunstanburgh, whose attempt to marry a man young enough to be her great-grandson has been the cause of this House's overthrow.'

She sat down, and the Duchess sprang to her feet, crying out that the House was insulted, and that these traitorous words should be taken down.

'We shall all be taken down ourselves,' replied the noble lady who had spoken, 'before many hours. Can we not devise some means of dying gracefully? At least let us spare ourselves the indignity of being hustled down the steps of Westminster Hall, as the unlucky Department of Police has been this morning hustled on Hampstead Heath.'

Several proposals were made. It was proposed to send a deputation of religion. But the Preaching Sisters had been rejected with scorn, when the army was still small and hesitating. What would happen, now that they were victorious? It was proposed that they should send a thousand girls, young, beautiful, and richly dressed, to make overtures of peace, and charm the men back to their allegiance. The young Lady Dunlop—aged eighteen—icily replied that they would not get ten girls to go on such an errand.

It was proposed, again, that they should send a messenger offering to treat preliminaries on Hampstead Hill. The messenger was despatched—she was the Clerk of the House—but she never came back.

Then the dreadful news arrived that the conqueror had assumed the title of King, and was marching with all his forces to Westminster, in order to take over the reins of power.

At this intelligence, which left nothing more to be expected but complete overthrow, the Peeresses cowered.

'As everything is gone,' said the middle-aged lady who had first expressed her opinion, 'and as the streets will be extremely uncomfortable until these men settle down, I shall go home and stay there. And I should recommend your ladyships to do the same, and to keep your daughters at home until they can learn to behave—as they have tried to make the men behave. My dears, submission belongs to the sex who do none of the work.'

She got up and went away, followed by about half the House. About a hundred Peeresses were left.

'I,' said the Duchess of Dunstanburgh, 'shall remain with the Chancellor till I am carried out.'

'I,' said the Chancellor, 'shall remain to protest against the invasion of armed men and the trampling upon law.'

'And I,' said young Lady Dunlop, loud enough to be heard all over the House, 'shall remain to see Lord Chester—I mean, His Majesty the King. He is a handsome fellow, and of course Constance will be his Queen.'

'Ladies,' said the Duchess, dignified and austere to the last, 'it is at least our duty to make a final stand for religion.'

Lady Dunlop scoffed. 'Religion!' she cried. 'Have we not had enough of that nonsense? Which of us believes any more in the Church? Even men have ceased to believe—especially since they were called upon to marry their grandmothers. The Perfect Woman! Why, we are ourselves the best educated, the best bred, the best born—and look at us! As for me, I shall go over to Lord Chester's religion, and in future worship the Perfect Man, if he likes to order it so.'

The Duchess made no reply. She had received so many insults; such dreadful things had been said; her cherished faiths, prejudices, and traditions had been so rudely attacked,—that all her forces were wanted to maintain her dignity. She sat now motionless, expectant, haggard. The game was played out. She had lost. She would have no more power.

It was then about half-past three in the afternoon. They waited in silence, these noble ladies, like the Senators of Rome when the Gaul was in the streets—without a word. Before long the tramp of feet and the clatter of arms were heard in Westminster Hall.

The very servants and officers, the clerks, of the House, had run away; there was not a woman in the place except themselves: the House looked deserted already.

There hung behind the Chancellor a heavy curtain rich with gold and lace: no one in that House had ever seen the curtain drawn. Yet it was known that behind it stood the image in marble of the only Sovereign acknowledged by the House—the Perfect Woman.

When the trampling of feet was heard in Westminster Hall, the Duchess of Dunstanburgh rose and slowly walked—she seemed ten years older—towards this curtain: when the doors of the House were thrown open violently, she stood beside the Chancellor, her hand upon the curtain.

Tan-ta-ra-ta-ra! A flourish of trumpets, and the trumpeters stood aside.

The Guards came after, marching up the floor of the House. They formed a lane. Then came the Bishop in his robes, preceded by his chaplain, the Rev. Clarence Veysey, surpliced, carrying a Book upon a velvet cushion; then the officers of the Staff with drawn swords; last, in splendid dress and flowing robes, the King himself.

As he entered, the Duchess drew aside the curtain and revealed, standing in pure white marble, with undraped limbs, wonderful beyond expression, the Heaven-descended figure of the Perfect Woman.

'Behold!' she cried. 'Revere the Divine Effigy of your Goddess.'

The young priest in surplice and cassock sprang upon the platform on which the figure stood and hurled it upon the floor. It fell upon the marble pavement with a crash.

'So fell the great God Dagon,' he cried.

Then no more remained. The ladies rose with a shriek, and in a moment the House was empty. It is not too much to say that the Duchess scuttled.

And while the King took his place upon the throne, the bands struck up again, the soldiers shouted, volleys of guns were fired for joy, and the bells were rung.

Strange to say, the dense crowd which gathered about the army of victory outside the Hall consisted almost wholly of women.

CONCLUSION

THE Great Revolution was thus accomplished. No woman was insulted: there was no pillage, no licence, no ill-treatment of anybody, no revenge. The long reign of woman, if it had not destroyed the natural ferocity and fighting energy of men, had at least taught them respect for the weaker sex.

The next steps, are they not written in the Books of the Chronicles of the country?

A few things remain to be noted.

Thus, because the streets were crowded with women come out to see, to lament, sometimes to curse, a proclamation was made ordering all women to keep within doors for the present, except such as were sent out to exercise children, and such as received permission for special purposes: they were forbidden the right of public meeting; the newspapers were stopped; religious worship of the old kind was prohibited.

These apparently harsh and arbitrary measures, tendered necessary by the refractory and mutinous conduct of the lower classes of women, who resented their deposition, were difficult to enforce, and required that every street should be garrisoned. To do this, thirty thousand additional men were needed: these were sent up by Jack Kennion, who had recruited double that number. As the women refused to obey, and it was impossible to use violence towards them, the men were ordered to turn the hose upon them. This had the desired effect; and a few draggled petticoats, lamentable in themselves, proved sufficient to clear the streets.

Then the word was given to bring out all the men and parade them in districts. Indeed, before this order, there were healthy and encouraging signs on all sides that the spirit of revolt was spreading even in the most secluded homes.

The men who formed the first army were entirely country born and bred. They had been accustomed to work together, and freedom became natural to them from the first. The men whom the Order of Council brought out of the houses of London were chiefly the men of the middle class—the most conventional, the worst educated, the least valuable of any. They lacked the physical advantages of the higher classes and of the lower; they were mostly, in spite of the laws for the Promotion of Health and Strength of Man, a puny, sickly race; they had been taught a trade, for instance, which it was not considered genteel to practice; they were not allowed to work at any occupation which brought in money, because it was foolishly considered ungentlemanly to work for money, or to invade, as it was called, woman's Province of Thought. Yet they had no money and no dot; they had very little hope of marrying; and mostly they lounged at home, peevish, unhappy, ignorantly craving for the life of occupation.

Yet when the day of deliverance came, they were almost forcibly dragged out of the house, showing the utmost reluctance to go, and clinging like children to their sisters and mothers. 'Alas!' cried the women, 'you will find yourselves among monsters and murderers, who have destroyed Religion and Government. Poor boys! What will be your fate?'

They were brought in companies of a hundred each before the officers of the Staff. At first they were turned out to camp in Hyde Park and other open places, where the best among them, finding themselves encouraged to cheerfulness, and in no way threatened or ill treated by these monsters, began to fraternise, to make friends, to practise gymnastics, to entertain rivalries, and in fact to enter into the body corporate. To such as these, who were quickly picked out from the ignoble herd, this new life appeared by no means disagreeable. They even began to listen to the words of the new Preachers, and the doctrines of the new Religion; they turned an obedient ear to the exhortations of those who exposed the inefficacy of the old Government. Finally, they were promoted to work of all kinds in the public departments, or were enlisted in the Army. It presently became the joy of these young fellows to go home and show their new ideas, their new manners, their new uniforms, and their new religion to the sisters whose rule they acknowledged no longer.

There came next the feeble youths who had not the courage to shake off the old chains, or the brains to adopt the new teaching. These poor creatures could not even fraternise; they knew not how to make friends. It was thought that their best chance was to be kept continually in barracks, there to work at the trade they had been taught, to eat at a common table, to live in common rooms, and to be made strong by physical exercise. Out of this poor material, however, very little good stuff could be made. In the long-run, they were chiefly turned into copying-clerks, the lowest and the meanest of all handicrafts.

Allusion has been made to the barracks in which were confined the unmarried men who had no friends to keep them. Among these were the poor creatures afflicted with some impediment to marriage, such as hump-back, crooked back, consumptive tendencies, threatenings of heart disease, cerebral affections, asthma, gout, and so forth. They were employed in houses of business at a very small rate of pay, receiving in return for their labour nothing for themselves but free board and lodging in the barracks. It is curious to relate that these poor fellows proved in the reorganisation of civic matters the most useful allies: they had lived so long together that they knew how to act together; they were so cheap as servants, and so good, that they had been entrusted with most important offices; in short, when the Government seemed about to fall to pieces by the threatened closing of all the mercantile houses, these honest fellows stepped to the front, took the reins, directed the banks, received the new men-clerks, taught and assigned their duties, and, in fine, carried on the trade of the country.

The question of religion was the greatest difficulty. Where were the preachers? There were but two or three in whom trust could be placed; and these, though they did their best, could not be everywhere at once. Therefore, for a while, the Religion of the Perfect Woman having been abolished, there seemed as if nothing else would take its place.

The Government for the present consisted of the titular King, who was not yet crowned, and the Council of State. There were no ministers, no departments, no Houses of Parliament. As regards the Lower House, it would have been unwise to elect it until the constituencies had learned by experience in local matters, something of the Art of Government. But the Upper? Consider that for two hundred years the title had descended through the mother to the eldest daughter. This being reversed, it became necessary to seek out the rightful heirs to the old titles by the male line. No titles were to be acknowledged except those which dated back to the old kings. These, which had been bestowed in obedience to the old laws, were to be claimed by their rightful owners. Now, it is easy to see that while a title held the female branches of the House together, because each would hope that the intervening claimants would drop out, the male branches would not be so careful to preserve their genealogies, and so a great many titles would be lost. This, indeed, proved to be the case, and out of the six hundred Peers who enjoyed their rank under Victoria of the nineteenth century, scarcely fifty were recovered. Many of these, too, were persons of quite humble rank, who had to be instructed in the simplest things before they were fit to wear a coronet.

All later titles were swept away together; nor was any woman allowed a title save by marriage, unless she was the daughter of a Duke, a Marquis, or an Earl, when she might bear a courtesy-title. Of course, the late Peeresses found themselves not only deprived of their power, but even of their very names; and it was the most cruel of all the misfortunes which befell the old Duchess of Dunstanburgh, that she found herself reduced from her splendid position to plain and simple Mrs Pendlebury, which had been the name of her third husband. All her estates went from her, and she retired to a first-floor lodging at Brighton, where she lived on the allowance made her by the Relief Commission appointed by Government for such cases as hers.

As regards public opinion on this and other changes, there was none, because Society was as yet not re-established; and the new daily papers were only feeling their way slowly to the expression of opinion. It remains to be told how these changes were received by the sex thus rudely set aside and deposed.

It cannot be denied that among the elders there was disaffection amounting to blind hatred. Yet what could they do? They could no longer combine; they had no papers; they had no club; they had no halls; they had no theatres for meeting; they had no discussion-forums,—as of old. Even they had no churches; and although in the past days they seldom went into a church, regarding religion as a thing belonging to men, they now made it their greatest grievance, that religion had been abolished. In private houses the worship of the Perfect Woman was long continued by those who had been brought up in that faith, and in days when it was actually believed in and accepted. As for the younger women, they, too, differed: The lower orders, for a long time, regretted their ancient liberty, when they could leave the husband to work in the house, children and all, and talk together the livelong day. But in time they came round. The middle-aged women, especially those of the professional classes, no doubt suffered greatly by being deprived of the work which was to them their chief pleasure. Some compensation was made to them by a system of partnership, in which practice in their own houses and private consultations were allowed some of them for life. As for the very young, it took a short time indeed to reconcile them to the change.

No more reading for professions! Hurrah! Did any girl ever really like reading law? No more drudgery in an office! Very well. Who would not prefer liberty and seeing the men work? They gave in with astonishing readiness to the new state of things. They ceased to grumble directly they realised what the change meant for them.

First, no anxiety about study, examinations, and a profession. Next, no responsibilities. Next, unlimited time to look after dress and matters of real importance. Then, no longer having to take things gravely on account of the weaker sex,—the men, who now took things merrily—even too merrily. Lastly, whereas no one was formerly allowed to marry unless she could support a husband and family, and then one had to go through all sorts of humiliating conferences with parents and guardians,—under the new régime every man seemed making love with all his might to every girl. Could anything be more delightful? Was it not infinitely better to be wooed and made love to when one was young, than to woo for oneself when one had already passed her best?

Then was born again that sweet feminine gift of coquetry: girls once more pretended to be cruel, whimsical, giddy, careless, and mischievous; the hard and anxious look vanished from their faces, and was replaced by sweet, soft smiles; flirtation was revived under another name—many names. A maiden loved to have half a dozen—yea, she did not mind half a hundred—dangling after her, or kneeling at her feet, men were taught that they must woo, not be wooed, and that a woman's love is not a thing to be had for the mere asking: and dancing was revived—real honest dancing of sweetheart and maid. There was laughter once more in the land; and all the songs were rewritten; and such pieces were enacted upon the stage as would but a month ago have taken everybody's breath away. And there was a general burning of silly books and bad pictures; and they began to open churches for the new Worship, and always more and more the image of the Divine Man filled woman's heart.

Finally, these things having been settled in the best way possible, it was resolved to hold the Coronation of the King at Westminster Abbey.

. . . .

'Constance,' he said holding her in his arms, 'you believe that I have always loved you, do you not?'

'I pray your Majesty,' she said, humbly, 'to forgive my errors of the past.'

'My dear, what is there to forgive?'

'Nay, now I know. There is the Perfect Woman; but she lives in the shadow of the Divine Man: she has her place in the Order of the World; but it is not the highest place. We reigned for a hundred years and more, and everything fell to pieces; you return, and all begins to advance again. It is as if the foot of woman destroyed the flowers which spring up beneath the foot of man. King, if I am to become your wife, I shall also become your most faithful subject.'

'You are my Queen,' he said; 'together we will reign: it may be for the good of our people. We have little strength of ourselves, but we seek it—love——'

'We seek it,' she replied, lifting her eyes to Heaven, 'of the Divine Man.'

. . . .

On the day of the Coronation, by Royal Order, all classes of the people were bidden to the ceremony; as many as could be admitted were invited to the Abbey. Along the line of march they had raised seats one above the other, covered with awnings. An innumerable crowd of people gathered at early morning, and took their places, waiting patiently for eleven, the hour of the procession.

At ten the Peers began to arrive—the newly recognised Peers—the men who had been brought up in ignorance of their origin and rank. They were uneasy in their robes and coronets; they had been carefully instructed in their part of the ceremony, but they were nervous. However, the people outside did not know this, and they cheered lustily.

Long before half-past ten there was not a vacant place in the Abbey; the venerable church was crowded with ladies, who were anxious to make the Coronation the point of a new departure; Society, it was said, would begin again with a King. No doubt, many ladies whispered, women were, after all, poor administrators; their nature was too tender, too much disposed to pity, which produced weakness. Men, who received these confessions, laughed courteously, but remembered the crowded prisons, and the prisoners, and the Convict Wardens.

At eleven o'clock the procession started from Buckingham Palace. The ancient ceremonials were copied as closely as possible. After the bands came the mounted Guards; then followed heralds; then came the Venerable Bishop of London, who was to crown the King, in a carriage; then officers of State on horseback; then the King's faithful Guards, those sturdy gamekeepers who stood by him at the beginning; and last of all, save for a regiment of cavalry which brought up the rear, the King himself on horseback—gallant, young, handsome, his face lit with the sunshine of success; and riding beside him—at sight of whom a shout went up that rent the air—no other than the beautiful Lady Carlyon herself.

It appeared, when they arrived at the Abbey, that the coronation was to be preceded by another and an unexpected ceremony. For the organ pealed forth the 'Wedding March'; there were waiting at the gates a dozen bridesmaids in white and silver; the choristers were ready with a wedding-hymn; and the Bishop, with the Very Rev. Clarence Veysey, newly appointed Dean of the Abbey, was within the altar-rails to make this illustrious pair man and wife.

Then followed, without pause, the Coronation service, with the braying of trumpets, the proclamation of heralds, the King's solemn oath, the crowning of King and Queen, and the homage of the Peers. And amid the shouts of the people, while cannon fired feux de joie, and the bells rang, and the bands played 'God save the King,' the newly-crowned monarch rode back to his Palace, bringing home with him the sweetheart of his childhood.

Now there is so much grace and virtue in a real love match that it goes straight to the heart of all who witness it. And since such fruits as these manifestly followed with Man's administration, not a maiden among them all but cried and waved her handkerchief, and sang 'God save the King!'

Made in the USA
Monee, IL
06 June 2024

59417536R00056